CLEO

CLEO
I Was, I Wasn't, I Am

DOYLE JOHNSON

iUniverse, Inc.
Bloomington

Cleo
I Was, I Wasn't, I Am

iUniverse books may be ordered through booksellers or by contacting:

iUniverse
1663 Liberty Drive
Bloomington, IN 47403
www.iuniverse.com
1-800-Authors (1-800-288-4677)

ISBN: 978-1-4620-1608-2 (sc)
ISBN: 978-1-4620-1607-5 (hc)
ISBN: 978-1-4620-1606-8 (e)

Library of Congress Control Number: 2011907622

Printed in the United States of America

iUniverse rev. date: 05/31/2011

1

The blood curdling, bone chilling scream came even before the thundering blast...

"Chad......!!"

Cleo Hertzwitz sat straight up, a strange and eerie silence gripped him. For a moment he sat there, his breath coming in short, hard gasps as if he'd been running. Shaking more from the dream than from the cold, it took several minutes of brisk rubbing and with the help of his hands flexing his knees, before he felt safe in assigning his legs the duty of propelling his body.

His thoughts going back to another time, but for now, a strong hunger pang gnawed at his gut, reminding him that certain things are required in order to keep the body alive, one was eating.

His worldly possessions consisted of one pair of jeans, very dirty with holes, one pullover sweat shirt, one pocket knife with a three and a half inch blade, a worn pocket rock with which to keep the blade razor sharp, one World War II GI overcoat, one sock cap, two socks with holes, one canvas and one leather shoe, all of which moved in unison with the man.

For many months now the hole he called home, dug with his hands and his knife, was located beneath the overpass at the rail yard in Mamelle. He had positioned it as close to the top of the incline as possible so only the train people had opportunity to see it. The long, hard digging last summer had finally paid off, now that it had grown bitterly cold. He seldom left his place until it was dark for fear of being discovered and dislodged.

Now his thoughts turned to Rico. Rico had come upon him one night as he was rummaging through the garbage behind *the Black Angus Steakhouse.*

"Senor, do you have no place to go?" Rico asked him; Cleo simply shook his head. "You wait maybe twenty minutes...I bring you something very good to eat." True to his word, Rico soon returned with a huge t-bone steak, cooked a bit too long for some discerning patron, a baked potato that was already prepared with only a little of it eaten, a styrofoam dish filled with peach cobbler, and a piping hot cup of coffee."You eat good senor, you come again; Rico work here every night."

It had been such a long time since he had said grace.

The garbage rack was located in the alley behind the steakhouse. There was room to crawl beneath if the alley had traffic, Cleo knew this well. Several times Ruis and Rogers, two night beat cops, had found him plundering there. Ruis relished the opportunity to inflict pain on anyone, especially the homeless. If he found Cleo in the alley, he would chase him, hitting him across the back and shoulders with his night stick, gleefully yelling something in Spanish Cleo could not understand.

It was with great trepidation and caution that he approached the top of the incline, then over the retaining cable and on to the alley. The alley was dark but Cleo knew it well. Just as he was getting to the garbage rack, headlights appeared at the end of the alley. He made a dash for the rack and no sooner made it before another car appeared at the other end of the alley. Fear gripped him. Surely it was Ruis and Roger, but God only knows who is in the other car. *This is my last day on this earth...* he thought. Ruis had made that very clear during the last beating.

The two cars drove within a few feet of each other and stopped, leaving the headlights on. Each driver emerged with a valise, meeting between the cars. Cleo could see them plainly now, it was not Ruis, Rogers, or anyone else he had ever seen. They were no more than a few feet from him as each man opened his valise and displayed its contents. He could hear them talking but couldn't understand the words. As they closed the valises and as if to exchange them, driver one quickly and adroitly drew a ten inch knife and before driver two could react, drove it to its hilt into his left side. A low, gurgling, guttural groan came from the driver's throat and he, out of sheer desperation, drew a Saturday Night Special from his pocket, fired, then crumpled to the ground as a melted candle. Unbelievably, the bullet found its mark, the two men died simultaneously.

Cleo crouched there, thoughts racing, *Are they dead? Was that money in the valise? Who knows where they are? Do I have time to get the valises and back to my place before the place is alive with cops?*

Quickly he crawled from his hiding, ran to the bodies of the dead men, grabbed the bags, ran down the alley, over the cable, and down the hill toward his hole. *I can't stay here,* he thought. Running, stumbling further down the hill, his feet became tangled in the old big coat and he fell, sprawling hands over head, a valise in each hand; neither came open.

Good merchandise, he thought.

As he made the tracks, a slow moving train was leaving the yard. Fortunately, there was enough glow from the city above enabling him to see an open door a few cars back. Trudging along with the train, he threw the valises aboard and managed to get on. *Now what,* came a sobering thought. He was shaking so hard he could barely lift the valises. Was he cold, scared, exhausted, or all of the above? He couldn't say.

In all the excitement his hunger had subsided, now the cold was a more pressing problem. If he didn't do something soon, he was going to freeze to death in that open boxcar. Finally, he managed to collect some loose packing material, raked it into a pile, put his feet beneath and in a fetal position, covered them with the bottom of his coat, pulled the collar over his head and lay very still...bags in hand, and eventually fell asleep.

2

"Has the jury reached a verdict?"

"We have, Your Honor."

"Will the foreman please read the verdict."

"We find for the plaintiff, the sum of $150,000 property damage and $100,000 punitive damages."

"Does the defendant wish to say anything?" the judge asked.

"No your Honor," his attorney answered.

Again Cleo was awakened abruptly, slowly realizing it was just another dream, causing him to relive those dreadful days and events.

Chad was an only child, bright, athletic and charming. His mother doted on him excessively. His achievements were many, making his parents very proud. There was Tee-Ball, pee wee league, little league, and the school play in which he had the leading part. As Chad reached puberty, his parents began to notice a change. They assumed it was his way of establishing independence. Soon it became evident there was more to it. He became withdrawn and seldom wanted to be in the presence of his parents. He had his own living quarters, a second garage located on the same property which was converted into living space for him. There was an intercom system installed by which he could both reach and be reached by the family in the main house. A similar structure, belonging to the neighbor, lay just behind Chad's. Those living there had never been very friendly, causing some concern for Chad's parents.

The telephone rang, a look at the clock revealed it was one forty-five in the morning. Shaking, the woman grabbed the receiver and said, "Hello."

"Is this Ms. Hertzwitz?" a strange voice asked.

"Yes!"

"This is Captain Flores at the police department. We have your son Chad and some others in custody; he's asked me to call and have you come to the station."

"What?? Why do you have Chad in custody?...We assumed he was in bed asleep."

"If you can come to the station, I'll be glad to discuss the situation with you." the captain said and hung up. Maggie sat, staring at the dead telephone, "Who was that?" Cleo asked in a troubled tone of voice.

"It was the police, they have Chad and asked us to come to the station." she said.

They dressed as quickly as possible and drove to the station. They walked inside where a very overweight man sat looking over some papers. He appeared to be ignoring the Hertzwitzes. Highly agitated, Maggie cleared her throat in an affirmative way.

The fat man, callously and indifferently, without looking up, asked, "Can I help you?"

Maggie felt a rage building she could hardly contain. "We're the Hertzwitzes to see a Captain Flores", she said.

"Have a seat ma'am, I'll see if he can see you" the fat man said, continuing to shuffle papers, he didn't look up or move--right away.

"It's two o'clock in the morning, they have our son and we'd like to see the captain right away, please!" Maggie insisted.

"Yes ma'am, please have a seat," he replied in a more authoritative voice.

Finally the indolent slob laboriously and with great difficulty, got up from his chair and disappeared into another room. Maggie became more and more frantic as the seconds seemed like hours. *What on earth could Chad have done to get himself arrested? Surely there has to be some mistake. As soon as we explain to the captain, we'll be able to take him home. Why doesn't he come tell us something?'* She wondered if the slob had gone somewhere and fallen asleep.

Finally the door opened, "The captain will see you now, this way please." He spoke as though he had said those same words a million times.

Captain Flores was a salt and pepper gray, fifty-five perhaps, dressed neatly in shirt and tie but without his coat. He rose to his feet as the Hertzwitzes entered the room. He extended his hand, took Maggie's and then Cleo's, "Let me say I'm sorry to have you come down here at this hour."

Anxiously Cleo asked, "What on earth is this all about? Is Chad hurt? Is he alright?"

"Oh, he's fine; no, he's not hurt. But first, before we get to yours, I have some questions of my own. Has Chad been in trouble with the law before?" he asked.

Quickly and in perfect harmony, they exclaimed, "Of course not!!!"

"How did a sixteen year-old boy happen to be out on the street at this time of morning?" the captain asked.

This time each waited for the other to answer; neither did... right away.

Finally Cleo said, "Sir, that's a question we're asking ourselves and don't have an answer. You see, he has his living quarters on our property but in a separate building. It's a long standing arrangement and has never been a problem. His custom is to come and say good night when he retires, but not every time. He doesn't have a car and no other means of transportation...we're baffled."

"Do you ever inspect his living quarters?" The captain asked.

"For what?", Cleo asked anxiously, "No, he wants his privacy, and we feel he's entitled to it. He brings his laundry to the house but does his own house cleaning."

"Have you noticed a change in Chad's personality---any change in his relationship with you as parents?" The captain watched the response of the parents very closely on this one. There was a long hesitation before either of them spoke.

"We have noticed a change, but didn't suspect there was anything wrong", Cleo said, defensively.

"Have you ever felt he wasn't telling the truth about something?" the captain asked.

"A few times," Maggie said, "but don't we all keep some things to ourselves?"

"Please don't be offended at the next question, but I have to ask. Have either of you ever used illegal drugs?"

Maggie's breath caught in her throat and for a moment felt as if she would pass out.

Cleo answered, his voice quivering said, "Heavens no! What kind of question is that? And what does it have to do..?" His voice trailed off as he realized the implication. *Oh NO! Surely not Chad*, his thoughts going so fast his head was swimming.

Maggie's pale complexion was such that the captain asked if he could get her a drink of water and she answered, "Yes."

The captain didn't immediately continue. It took Maggie a few minutes to compose herself. She took a sip of the water he offered and found it difficult to swallow.

Finally Cleo said, "Can you describe the situation for us? Can we take Chad home now?"

"I'm afraid it's not quite that simple," Flores said, "these boys are in some serious trouble. Nothing can be done until we can go before a judge and that'll be sometime later this morning. As to why they were brought in, the boys were pulled over for speeding. It's standard procedure, if the officers are suspicious, they give the drug dog a trip around the car, if he indicates there are drugs aboard, the officers then have a legal right to search. Upon the examination of the car, officers found a considerable amount of meth and cocaine and we suspect they were on their way to deliver it."

"You keep saying they--who are 'they'?!" Cleo asked irritably.

Flores, keeping his voice calm and with Maggie in mind said,

"There were four boys in the car. I can't reveal the names of the others because they are minors. I can give you their ages according to their ID's. One of the boys, the driver of the car is seventeen; two of the others are sixteen. Chad is sixteen, is that right?"

Maggie nodded, the paper cup shaking so as to spill its contents.

"Can you give us an idea what to expect now?" Cleo asked.

"Of course it will depend on the judge. The prosecutor will most likely charge them with possession with intent to deliver; that's a felony. The judge will then decide what to do. Usually, if they have not had prior offenses, he'll set their bond at $25,000 each and remand them to the custody of their parents". At that news, the paper cup collapsed in Maggie's hands, the contents spilling on the floor. Maggie lost her composure--the captain was not impressed.

3

Rico heard the shot and the noise out back and opened the door in time to see a fleeing individual wearing a dirty overcoat with a valise in each hand and two men lying dead between two cars facing each other. What on earth could all this mean? Could a man whom he had befriended, somehow be involved?

Soon the alley was alive with cops, sirens blasting, emergency lights flashing, along with a crowd of onlookers.

One of the officers yelled, "Did anyone see what happened?" When no one answered, "Do any of you know these men?" Still no one answered. Then, "If you're not part of this investigation, get out of here now or you'll find yourself at headquarters trying to make someone believe you had nothing to do with this crime!"

Rico quietly retreated to the kitchen, not willing to implicate his friend just yet.

As the officers worked to secure the crime scene, Watson, the chief investigator, turned to Sgt. Radley and said, "There's more to this than meets the eye; there's something missing. It has all the markings of a drug deal gone bad, but where's the money? Where are the drugs?" Pausing briefly, he said, " Seal off the area, get the coroner down here, and get in touch with Chief Browning."

Chuck Browning, 53 years old and with the police force for more than thirty years, twenty five of those in homicide. He joined the force fresh out of college and soon became noted for his astute perception. Arriving at the scene, "Anyone see anything?" he asked.

"No one will say anything." Watson said.

"Do any of you know of any regular, illegal activity in this particular alley?" Browning asked, turning to the officers. No one responded.

The coroner arrived and pronounced both men dead after which they were taken to the morgue.

"Watson, stay on this, get these men's I.D. as soon as possible," Browning said, "Have these cars taken to the pound and sealed until I can go over them.

"Right, Chief."

4

❦

Cleo awoke and found the train stopped. Although it was cold here, he realized it was warmer than where he'd been. Near morning now, he could see lights of a town a short distance away. He began to stand, and for a moment thought he wouldn't be able. After taking a few steps in the boxcar, everything seemed to be working. He focused his attention on the briefcases. *What is in there that cost two men their lives?* He pondered, as he decided to take a look. But try as he would he could not get them open. It occurred to him he had to find a way to hide them until he was more familiar with the area. A man of his appearance, with two very expensive briefcases, would certainly arouse the curiosity of the cops.

He couldn't remember when he had bathed, certainly not since winter set in and it had been even longer since he'd shaved or had his hair cut.

Leaving the train, looking both ways, toward the rear he saw a bridge spanning a small creek. Being familiar with such a place, he made his way to it. Under the bridge, huge rocks lay against the bank to prevent erosion.

He decided by removing few of the rocks from the top, (and with the help of his knife), might dig a hole large enough for one of the valises and then replace the rocks. He decided to keep them in separate location.

He began chipping away at the dirt, carefully removing it one handful at a time, throwing it into the water so as not to leave evidence of his activity. It took longer than he had anticipated, but at last one of the bags was secured. Going top side, repeating the process, he began removing the rocks between the ties, between the rails.

Finally the job was done. Satisfied with it, his thoughts turned to himself. He cleaned his knife at the creek, took the stone and began sharpening it.

Unburdened by the valises, he began to trudge toward the town. Although it was daylight now, he would draw no more attention than any other tramp. Passing along a salvage yard, he saw a sign that read: WE BUY JUNK. A thought came to him: maybe he could find enough junk iron to earn the price of a sandwich.

A railroad spike here and there, carried in the pockets of the old coat, was enough to test his plan. The business was just opening as he approached the office of the salvage yard.

"Can I help you?" the man asked.

"I'm afraid I don't have much junk, but maybe enough to buy a sandwich?" He unloaded his pockets on the counter.

The man stared in disbelief. "Where you coming from buddy?"

"Here and there—nowhere and everywhere; I'm homeless."

"Are you running?"

"No!" Cleo said, slightly lying. "I apologize for my appearance but there are few places for guys like me to clean up. Our primary concern is finding food."

"When did you last eat?"

"I'm not sure but it's been a few days," he said.

"Are you willing to work for a meal?" the man asked.

"Yes sir!"

"Tell you what, my yard man called in sick, if you're willing to help me today, I'll see that you're well fed," the man said, as he looked Cleo over.

"I thank you for your offer—I'm ready when you are." Cleo said.

"First, you have to get rid of that old big coat, you can't work in that." Looking down at the man's feet, asked, "What size shoe do you wear?"

"Eleven and a half" Cleo answered.

He reached beneath the counter and pulled out a pair of shoes, "Well, here's a pair I've discarded, they're not much, but they beat what you have on."

The owner then picked up the phone and dialed, "Patty, fix a big breakfast and bring it to the office. Look in the closet and bring one of my old coats with you--bring a pair of socks." After a pause he said, "I'll explain when you get here," hung up, and turned to Cleo,

"My name's Jeb Clancy, I own the business. My dad opened it forty- three years ago. I grew up in the junk business."

With a slight tilt of the head and a quizzical look, he continued, "Do you follow orders well?" he asked.

"Yes sir," he said, "…my name is Cleo Hertzwitz."

"Things have to be done a certain way. I'll show you what I want you to do." Jeb continued.

Walking through the salvage yard, Jeb pointed out the different types of metal, and how they were to be sorted.

Jeb said, "You have to be firm, people are interested only in getting the stuff off their rig, you have to insist on them unloading in the right places."

Back in the office, Patty soon arrived with the food, socks and coat. "This is my wife Patty. Patty, this is Cleo Hertzwitz."

What on earth is this, Patty thought as she put the food on a table and poured the coffee.

Cleo managed to eat without gulping, but it was very difficult. Never had he tasted anything so good! Finishing the last morsel and the last drop of coffee Cleo said, "Thank you is all I can say now, but I'll repay your kindness somehow."

He went to the bathroom and for the first time in a long time, saw himself in the mirror, a sight he could hardly believe! As he worked to clean himself up a bit, he overheard the conversation in the office.

"Where on earth did you come up with this guy?" Patty asked, "This is a recipe for disaster."

"How do you turn away a hungry man?" Jeb asked, "Besides, didn't you enjoy seeing him inhale his food?"

After junking the old coat, Cleo washed himself as well as he could, put on his 'new' shoes, and after a long time, with the help of lot of water, managed to get a comb through his filthy hair.

Feeling a little refreshed, he joined Jeb and Patty. "I'm as ready as I'll ever be," he said. Jeb and Patty could only smile.

The first customer pulled up on the scales and Cleo went for the four-wheeler. Pulling alongside of the customer and inspecting the cargo he said, "Follow me please." With that Cleo was earning his pay.

At lunch time, Patty again brought food and coffee. After eating, Patty said, "I found some clothes that Jeb doesn't wear anymore and since you two are near the same size, I brought them to see if you would like to have them." It wasn't hard to decide. Cleo's head was spinning, just a few hours ago he was afraid to be seen, but now......

5

The memory of Chad was his constant companion. *Why didn't he learn?* Cleo asked himself. Soon after his trial, he was back with his old friends, doing the same things. It was that which ended his life. He was killed instantly by a blast, created by his attempt to manufacture meth.

After his funeral, Maggie completely withdrew from everything and everybody. She spent most of her time in her bedroom, refusing to communicate with anyone, even Cleo. After rising and making coffee, Cleo went to her room to check on her. It was not a big surprise that she didn't answer his knock, and he wasn't shocked at what he found when he entered the room: the empty pill bottles, the ghost like figure, neither moving nor breathing; He called her name but didn't expect an answer.

For the longest time, Cleo just sat on the side of her bed, holding her hand, thoughts running through his mind, *How did we get from a happy family to nothing more than a broken man with seemingly no way to turn?*

His job of personnel manager at the plant now meant nothing. All the plans and anticipation for the future died with his wife and son.

A week later Cleo called the lawyer who had defended him, told him to bring the necessary papers and he would sign everything over to him; if there was something left after satisfying the court, that would be his fee. With a small amount of cash, Cleo got into the family car, began driving, having no notion where he was going, nor caring. With that, Cleo Hertzwitz became a homeless individual.

6

The I.D.s of the two dead men were of little help, neither were wanted; rap sheets revealed gang participation and drug trafficking but they appeared to be low level thugs.

"Someone's here to see you Rico." His boss said, motioning to his office. A detective sitting next to the desk, pointed to a chair, said to Rico,

"Have a seat. I'm Dan Watson of the downtown precinct. A few days ago, there was a double murder behind the steakhouse; were you working that night?"

"Si senor, I work five nights each week."

"Did you see or hear anything that night?"

"No senor! Rico see nahthink."

"Rico, murder is a serious offense, a person can become involved in a case simply by having information concerning the crime. If you have any such information, I urge you to tell us what you know." Watson continued. Rico sat motionless.

"One of the night cops, I believe his name is Ruis, tells us that some tramp frequents the garbage area. Do you know anything of that?" Watson asked. Rico now became very nervous, if he tells what he knows, he might lose his job for feeding someone out the back door; if he doesn't, he might be in trouble with the law.

"Rico, do you know of this man?" Watson insisted.

"Si! There was such a man. He sometime come at night; he is good man, no kill anyone."

"Have you seen this man since the murder?"

"No senor."

"Do you know his name or where he lives?"

"No senor."

"Have you ever seen another person with this guy?"

"No senor!"

"Have you known of people being in the alley at night before?"

"No senor, only this man."

Rico prayed the detective would not ask him if he saw this man the night of the murder. Unbelievably, his prayer was answered.

After a long pause, Watson said, "Thank you Rico for your cooperation. If you happen to see this man again, please have him get in touch with us."

After dismissing Rico, Watson turned to the restaurant owner and said, "I think he knows more than he's telling."

"Do you think he is somehow involved?" the owner asked.

"No, not directly but he may be trying to protect someone who is."

7

As the day began to draw to a close, Jeb and Cleo were discussing the business of the day when Jeb's curiosity overcame him.

"What are your plans, Cleo? Where do you go from here?" Jeb asked.

"Where do I go from here?" Cleo mused seriously. "You know Jeb, when I showed up at your place this morning, I might have given you a much different answer. I have to tell you, no matter how long I live or where I go, I'll remember this day forever. Earlier you ask me where I was coming from . There was a lot contained in my reply, not only with regard to where I am or where I'm going, but what's in my soul. I once had a wife, a son, a home and was fairly well off, all of which came to an abrupt end. My son died from an explosion which resulted as he was attempting to manufacture methamphetamine. My wife, Maggie, was so wrapped up in our son that she simply was unable to go on. Five days after my son's funeral, Maggie took her own life. I was sued as a result of the blast which damaged some of our neighbor's property and the settlement took everything I had."

Cleo paused as those old events came calling once again, then continued, "I gave my lawyer power of attorney and then just left. I have no close relatives; certainly none that care where I am. For these many months, I have been aimless, without a friend in which to confide, no companion, with one brief exception, no earthly possessions and no concern for anything or anybody. I felt like a 'key to a lock which had been changed'. It was as if I were the only person on earth. Your kindness, and I think to some extent, your understanding, has resurrected something inside of me that had died. I reckon I can't describe the feeling of actually working and being productive. I thank you for the clothes, the food and for your generosity. But most of all, I thank you for the opportunity to speak man to man with someone."

There was a lengthy silence, "First of all, may I say I'm sorry for your misfortune," Jeb said, "When I saw you for the first time I thought you were the most pitiful sight I'd ever seen. To tell you the truth, my first inclination was to tell you to get lost."

Again, Jeb paused --wondering how to continue, finally said, "Cleo, I want to make you a proposition. I have observed you today, and I'd like to help you. If you'd like to stay and work for a week, time enough to get back into the swing of things, I'll pay you my going wage. I'll even advance you a $100 to get yourself squared away. I'll take you to town for some underwear, socks, shaving equipment and whatever you need, Patty can give you a haircut if you'd like."

Both men simply looked at each other for several moments; Cleo not believing what he had just heard; Jeb thinking, *this man has pride.* Finally Jeb continued, "If you're interested, we have to find a place for you to stay. There's a mission on the other side of town that'll put you up for a few days. As for getting to work, I'll come by and pick you up. We'll try this for a week. That'll give you an opportunity to consider everything more fully.

"Of course I accept! I can only say I'm astounded; I can hardly take it in." Cleo said as he tried hard to keep from showing his delight, "What about your other helper?"

"There's enough for the two of you." Jeb assured him.

Later, Jeb secured him a place to stay at the mission and Patty did his shopping. Afterwards she cut his hair, all the time asking herself, w*hy are we doing this? We know nothing of the guy and we've taken him in as though he were a relative.*

At the mission, Cleo was assigned a bed and given the rules of the mission.

"Your privilege of staying here is contingent upon your abiding by these rules; there are no exceptions. Breakfast is at 6:30, be there or miss out." the rather stout lady informed him. It had been a long time since he had enjoyed a warm shower or sat at a table with food on it.

Next morning as Jeb and Cleo arrived at the business, a young man was standing with the gate open. Jeb parked and as the three walked toward the office Jeb said, "Cleo, this is my other helper Tony Belcher; Tony, this is Cleo Hertzwitz. He'll be helping us out for a while." The two men shook hands but resentment was written all over Tony's face.

"I'm glad to meet you Tony," Cleo said. Tony just turned away without responding.

Jeb, a little embarrassed, said, "He'll liven up after a while, don't pay any attention to him."

Resentment grew as the day progressed, Tony hardly spoke at all and when he did, it was very vitriolic. Cleo tried to avoid him as much as possible, not wanting to create an unpleasant situation. It was very obvious Tony was never going to be a friend to Cleo.

At the end of the week Jeb called Cleo in the office. "Have a seat and let's talk. First, tell me what you're thinking?"

"I'm sorry—have I done something wrong?"

"Oh no! Quite the contrary!" Jeb said, "You've done a very good job. I'm prepared to offer you a permanent job if you're interested. With your work skills you could do much better and if you want to move on I'll understand."

Cleo sat for several moments without speaking. *The briefcases— what about the briefcases?* He hadn't had opportunity to check on them. *Should I divulge their existence and whereabouts? How will this affect the offer this man has just made?*

He decided not to tell.

Finally he began, "Jeb, you have been so good and considerate of me, I hardly know what to say. If I accept your offer, I have a lot of things to consider: I have to find a place to live, to get some kind of transportation, maybe a bike. I have to buy some clothes if I'm to be presentable at the business." Again he paused, bringing a slight smile from Jeb. Then he continued, "But if you can tolerate my situation, I humbly accept your kind offer."

He was greatly troubled by keeping the briefcases a secret, knowing at some time Jeb would have to know and the longer it was put off, the harder it would be both for Cleo and Jeb: Cleo to explain and Jeb to understand or be disappointed, maybe damaging the relationship forever.

"We can find you a room at a boarding house," Jeb said, jolting Cleo back to reality. "Your week's salary will be sufficient for that with some left over for food. As for transportation, I'll continue to pick you up for a couple more weeks and the clothes can wait."

The boarding house wasn't the home he'd had before, but at last Cleo had a place of his own.

Jeb's friendly gesture caused Cleo to think of Rico. *Tomorrow I'll send him a card.*

8

As Rico was approaching the Steak House for work, a car pulled up beside him, a sinister character jumped from the car, grabbed Rico, shoved him in, crawled in behind, and the driver sped away. The thug immediately pulled a hood over Rico's head.

"Senor, I must get to work, what you want from me, I have no money?"

"Don't ask questions", the man said.

Rico became very frightened, thinking he'd be killed. Eventually they came to a stop. The thug climbed out, took Rico by the collar and forced him inside. Once inside, the smell of cigar smoke was very rank. The hood was not removed.

"Sidown Mr. Rico," some character demanded, "maybe you wonder how I know your name?"

Rico was too scared to reply. *Who is this,* Rico thought; *I think I hear him before—but where?*

"We're going to ask you some questions and we know you know the answers. We have ways of persuading you to tell us what we want to know." The thug jerked Rico to his feet, then roughly pulled a cuff around his ankle, tied his feet together and backed away.

Suddenly Rico cried out as a wave of electricity surged through his body, "Please! Senor! Don't kill Rico."

"If the answers to our question are true, you won't feel anything, but if not, the shocks will just get stronger. Believe me, it's not pretty" the thug said.

Interrupting Rico's thoughts, the man continued, "Recently a double murder occurred behind the place where you work. There were some very valuable things in the possession of each of these men-- they were not found. We have reason to believe you have information which will help us locate these items."

"Senor, I tell policeman everything!"

Suddenly another scream erupted from Rico. "Please Senor! I tell you all I know!"

"No, we are convinced you didn't tell everything," the man said emphatically. "We believe you have more knowledge of the old tramp you've been feeding. We want to know everything you know about this man: his name, where he lives, what he does, and if he has someone that hangs out with him."

"Senor, I know nothing of this."

Again a belt of electricity surged through his body. By now Rico was shaking uncontrollably. "Please Senor! I find him looking for food in the garbage and fix him discarded food. I not know name, I not know where he live, he come up from trains, it all I know." Rico said becoming more and more agonized.

"This is a most important question, take time to think it over before you answer. Your well-being is at stake. Did you see this man the night of the murders?" the thug asked.

Without hesitation, "Yes sir, I see him running toward trains with suitcases." Rico replied, as he wondered if he would ever see his place of work again.

"Have you seen this individual since the killing?"

"No senor, no see."

"Remove the bracelet Beast, drive him back to the Steak House." The thug turned to Rico and said, "If you value your health and well-being, you will not—I repeat, will not mention this meeting to anyone. Do you understand?"

"Si Senor." Rico managed to say, wondering all the while, *Will they really take me back or are they going to kill me?*

Eventually the car came to a stop and the thug pulled Rico from the car. "Stand very still," he said "do not remove the hood until you count to twenty." The car sped away and Rico began to count.

9

Chief Browning called detective Watson in his office for an update on the killings. "Have a seat Watson. How's the family?"

"Good shape." Watson said as he selected one of the plush chairs.

"Tell me, how's the investigation of the double murder coming along, anything new?"

"Not much Sir, we have identified the two men but that didn't reveal much, so far as we can tell. We are convinced it was a drug deal gone bad. Both murder weapons were found at the scene, which tells us there is at least one other individual somehow involved. Our only lead to who that might be, is the old tramp that hung around the back of the restaurant. If he is involved, it's very puzzling. Ruis, one of the night cops, says he's run him away from the area several times. The one fact that keeps the tramp as a 'person of interest' is that he hasn't been seen since the event took place."

"Is the area being watched?" Browning asked as he tapped his hand with a pencil. "If it was a bad drug deal, you know there are other people interested in the missing items. I believe, at some point, they will come for the kid."

After a brief silence, the chief continued, "Those folks are not bound by scruples; if they get a lead, extreme measures will be taken to get their hands on whoever is responsible for the disappearance of the goods. It seems to me this kid is going to be a target for the goons. I suggest we watch him a few days. If my hunch is correct, someone is going to find this kid and if he doesn't give them the information they're looking for, he is apt to become buzzard bait."

"I'll get some men on it immediately and keep you posted." Watson said, shook hands with the Chief and left the room.

10

The owner of the restaurant, known as *'BAS'*, (an acronym for **B**lack **A**ngus **S**teakhouse,) yelled, "Hey Rico! You got mail!"

Rico took the envelope addressed to the *Black Angus Steakhouse, attention Rico*. He tore open the envelope and removed the card which read: *"From a friend who will never forget. Thanks for the lift, Mi Amigo."* A quizzical look came over his face. There was no name, no return address; the only clue was the postmark. Rico was sure he knew no one in that city.

Bas stayed while Rico opened the envelope and read the message. Seeing the expression on Rico's face, he became curious.

"Who's it from?" he asked.

Rico, still perplexed, shrugged his shoulders and went back to the kitchen. *It has to be from the tramp! But where is he now? What if they find out it's from him? Will I be in more trouble?*

Visibly upset, he continued his work. In so doing he knocked a tray of dirty dishes off the table, spilling uneaten food and drinks all over. In his haste to clean up the mess, he cut himself on a broken piece of glass. As was policy, he had to report the incident, treat it and leave the premises.

Bas, hearing the crash went to investigate. He sent Rico to the office where the secretary could tend to his wound. Curiosity was impelling, there on the table lay the envelope. *What's in that card that upset Rico so? Should I investigate? Should I violate his privacy?*' All the while he was making his way to the envelope.

As soon as he'd read the message and the postmark he picked up the phone. "We need to meet---there are new developments. Be at the shop at 8 o'clock tonight."

Bas gave Ruis the card and said nothing until he had read it.

"This has to be from the tramp. Think we could find this guy if we go down there?" Bas asked.

After deliberating for a moment, Ruis, (known as Lucky in some circles) said, "I have some vacation coming; it'll take me a couple of days to get it arranged—I'll call you." The two shook hands, and Bas went one way, ten minutes later Lucky went in the other direction. Careful not to be seen, Bas returned the envelope.

Having dark skin, and with professionally applied cosmetics, along with an appropriate hair piece, Lucky now became African American. A phone call and he was on his way.

Arriving late in the evening, he pulled into a restaurant with a large, flashing neon sign which read, ***Ricky's***. Inside, he took a booth and placed his order. After finishing his meal, ,"My compliments to the chef; a very fine dinner indeed," he said to the cashier, "I'd like to show my appreciation ." pulling off a twenty from a very large and conspicuous roll, "For the chef," paid his bill, then with another twenty, "For the waiter," and left the building.

Next morning Lucky was at Ricky's early, as was his plan. Again he was very complimentary and generous, prompting the cashier to say, "Obviously, you're not from around here; we appreciate your dining with us."

"No, I'm from Marmelle-- north a couple hundred miles. My name is D.C. Wallace (giving his ficticious identity) and I'm in town looking for an individual on a personal matter. You seem to be very perceptive, do you regularly notice people who are—'not from around here'?"

"Reasonably so I guess." She answered.

"Is there anyone that stands out in your mind within the last few weeks?" He asked.

"No. I can't say there is," she said.

"Is there a mission or a place where a homeless person might find a meal and a bed?" he continued. She gave him direction to the mission.

At the mission Lucky approached the lady at the desk, "I'm D.C.Wallace from Marmelle, I'm in town looking for an individual. I wonder if you might help?"

The woman gave him an incredulous, somewhat snide look,

"Has there been someone here looking for a handout in the last few weeks that maybe stands out in your mind?"

"Mister, it's obvious you don't know much about homeless people," the stout lady said, without so much as a 'may I help you', "here, they come and go more than in Grand Central Station. Some leave after a meal, some next day, others stay the maximum. Even if I knew who you're looking for, our rules forbid me revealing anything about these people. Good day Sir."

Lucky wondered what her mother was like. His thoughts continued, *If it was the tramp that sent the card to Rico and if he's still in St Ann, he's either tapped the briefcase for money or he has a job.*

11

⚘

Jeb and Patty had just finished their dinner at Ricky's and were having a glass of wine when some friends, Jack and Fran Staton, came in and joined them. After a few amenities the conversation got around to business.

"How goes it?" Jack asked.

"I'm doing very well I guess."

"Ask him about his new help." Patty said chidingly. Jack turned to Jeb and waited for an answer.

"Patty can't seem to get past my hiring a guy about whom I know so very little. He showed up at my place a few days ago, the most pitiful sight I've seen in a long time. He brought in a few railroad spikes and a piece of flat iron and asked if it was enough to buy a sandwich. I ask him if he was willing to work for a meal and he quickly said 'yes.' We cleaned him up a little and Patty brought him some breakfast. One didn't have to wonder if he was truly hungry. Well, true to his word, he worked diligently all day; I was more than a little impressed and offered to let him continue for the rest of the week."

After a brief pause, Jeb continued, "It became obvious, this man had not always been a tramp. At the end of the week, I asked him what plans he had. Basically, he didn't have plans. It was at that point he told me the story. His only son was killed in an accident, which resulted in him being sued; the settlement was simply overwhelming, leaving him penniless. His wife, unable to cope with the loss of the son, took her own life."

Jeb paused; Jack remained silent. After a few moments Jeb continued. "I don't know if I have a soft spot, but I felt almost compelled to help this man. He is an excellent worker-- one that doesn't require constant oversight. Anyway, I offered to hire him if he was willing and he, seemingly humiliated, accepted my offer."

Next to their table sat an African American gentleman who seemed to be quite interested in their conversation. After the foursome finished, paid their bill and left, Lucky went to the cashier to inquire of their indentities. Of course, the cashier was more than willing to reveal it.

Bas's cell made the beep and the message read: *Have located subject--- subject is unaware of my presence. Need a tail-- Jim 'The Psychic' will do- no indication of items' location.*

Bas got in touch with Jim and arranged a meeting. "Jim, we have a real problem. As you know, two men were killed a few days ago; exactly how all that came down is somewhat of a mystery. A sizable amount of coke and $150,000.00 cash disappeared. The only clue we have is a old tramp that hung out in the alley where the two were killed. After the murders, the tramp disappeared. We think he is the key to solving this thing and the recovery of the merchandise. We think Lucky has located the old tramp in St Ann, a town a couple hundred miles to the south. We need you to tail him for a few days in hopes he'll reveal the whereabouts of the goods. When you get into town, Lucky suggests you meet him at Ricky's restaurant and formulate a plan."

"I'll be there in four hours," Jim said. "Is there anything else I should know before I talk to Lucky?"

"I don't need to remind you, this is a very sensitive situation, a slip-up could cause heads to roll" Bas said, peeling off ten $100.00 bills, to which Jim said, "I'm on my way."

Jim arrived at Ricky's, the hostess asked, "One?"

Jim answered, "I'm to meet a Mr. D.C . Wallace?"

"Yes, he's expecting you- this way please." The two men shook hands as the hostess left.

"What's the situation?" Jim asked as they took their seats.

"I assume you know of the murders of two of our men?" began D.C. "a considerable amount of money and merchandise is missing. We have reason to believe the individual you are to observe has something to do with that disappearance. I've been here a couple of days and have located him. He is employed by a junk dealer across town. I overheard his boss and some others discussing him and his transition from a tramp to a valuable employee. Our approach to this matter must be very delicate. We know almost nothing of this guy, nothing of his background, nothing of his contacts. We don't know for sure that he has the stuff! Tail him for two or three days, try to find out if he has it in his possession or stashed away. Don't make contact with him. I have to return to work but keep me up to date on your progress, be discrete; texting is the safest way." The two men left the restaurant together.

12

Again the Chief called Watson in for an update. "Any progress?" Browning asked.

"Not much chief."

"Watson," the chief said rather abruptly, "What do we know about the two victims? Do we know if they are local?"

"We're trying to ascertain their origin." Watson replied sheepishly, "We know that drugs are being smuggled in, but this is the closest thing we've had to putting our hands on anything. You know the smugglers find the most obscure people to deliver this stuff, thus, it's more difficult to trace them."

"How about receivers? Are there any suspects----anyone you're watching?" Browning asked.

Looking away Watson replied, "Honestly, we have very little evidence with which to base our investigation."

The chief said as he rose from his chair and offered Watson his hand, "The difficulty is understandable; it's not often the subjects are both killers and victims. Nevertheless, a good challenge is healthy. The answer will come and likely from an unexpected source, so often that's the case. Keep me posted, if I can assist you in any way, just call."

"Thank you chief, I'll do just that." And with that he shook the chief's hand and left.

After dismissing Watson the Chief rang Bas, "This is Chief Browning."

"Yes Sir, how can I help you?" Bas asked.

"I'd like to talk with the kid again. Can you get him down here? It shouldn't take long"

"When do you want him?" Bas asked.

"I'm ready now if it's convenient." The Chief said and hung up.

Rico had just walked into the restaurant for work. Bas called out, "Rico! Come go with me, the Chief wants to see us."

Rico became agitated thinking he is in trouble plenty. "Why Chief want to see me?" he asked.

"He didn't say." Bas said in a condescending tone.

"Come in Rico and have a seat. I assure you, you are not in any trouble," the Chief said, recognizing Rico's anxiety. "We're still trying to solve the mystery of the two guys that were killed behind your work. Often, early interviews are incomplete. Sometimes, as leads are developed they prompt further questions. Has anyone besides the police contacted you since that night?"

Rico became unsettled and the color left his face.

The Chief repeated the question, "Has anyone besides the police contacted you since that night?"

"Rico very much afraid!" he said, "Man say no tell anyone."

"What man?" asked the Chief.

"Rico don' know, I no see him."

"You have to explain that," the Chief said. "How could you talk to someone without seeing him? Were you talking to him on the phone?"

"No Senor, I come one night to work, some man come from car, grab me, pushed me in car, put cover over my head, I no see anyone. We go somewhere, I don' know. They put somethin' on Rico leg, then come big shock. Another man asked me questions. They no take cover off my head. He asked if I know the man who come up from the trains, if I see him since murder, I say no, then shock come again! I tell him I see man run away with two suitcases. I don' see this man from trains anymore. He say if I tell of meeting he hurt Rico bad. They drive me back where I work and say no take off cover 'til I count twenty. When I count twenty and take off cover, there was no one. Rico scared."

"Is there anything more you can tell me?" the chief asked, "Anything at all?"

Again Rico became very nervous. It was obvious he had more information.

"Rico, I understand you being scared, but the police will make every effort to keep you safe. But we can do that so much better if we round up these guys and put them away. If you have any information that you haven't given me, for your own safety, tell me."

"I don' know of this, but I get card from someone I don' know; from town I don' know. Card say, *'From a friend who will never forget. Thanks for the lift, Mi Amigo.'* I dunno, it no give name."

"Did anyone else see your card?" the Chief asked.

"I dunno, I cut finger and have to leave work. Maybe someone see it."

"Do you still have the card"

"Si"

"Do you mind if I take a look at it?"

"No, I don' mind, I don' have it now, card is at work."

"May I come by later and take a look?"

"Si".

After Rico left the Chief, still terrified, he thought ,*What if bad men know I tell? Maybe they see me go to police.*

As they drove back to the restaurant, Bas asked, "Are you sure you want to give the chief your card? You don't have to you know."

"I don' know! I scared! You give Rico his money today?"

"Yes, you can take your card too." the manager said as they pulled into the parking lot.

Rico got his check, stopped at the cashier, went to his apartment, threw his belongings in the old cloth bag, paid his rent and rapidly went to the bus station.

" I go this town," showing the ticket agent the postmark on the card.

"One way or round trip?" the agent asked.

"I don' know one way or round trip"? Rico said.

"Are you coming back or are you staying?" he asked.

"Rico no come back."

"That'll be $42.50," the agent said callously, and gave Rico the ticket south. He boarded the bus, nervously looking over the other passengers, walked to the back of the bus and took a seat. Reality closed in. *What I do? How do I get job? Where I stay?* he thought. Finally he fell asleep

13

The driver shook Rico, "Hey buddy, this is your stop."

Momentarily disoriented, he jumped to his feet, slowly remembering where he was, reached above, retrieved his bag, and made his way off the bus.

Unfamiliar with his surroundings, he simply began to walk. He'd not gone far before a police cruiser pulled along side of him.

"Good evening" the officer said, "where're you headed?

"I don' know, I come to this town, maybe find my friend."

"What's your friend's name?"

"I don' know name."

"You come here looking for a friend whose name you don't know?"

"Si Senor."

"Do you have identification?"

"Si" and gave him his picture I.D. which read Rico Gonzales, age 23, race Latino.

"Where are you staying?" the officer inquired.

"I don' know where I stay." Rico said.

"Maybe we better go to the station and check out some things. Turn around and put your hands behind you." The officer said.

"What Rico do?, I no bad man." He said.

"I know, but we have to check out some things and then you can go," the officer said as he opened the back door of the crusier. "Please have a seat."

Forty five minutes later and answers to many questions, the officer said, "You're free to go."

"Where find sleep place?" Rico asked. The sergeant told the officer to take him to the mission. At the mission, the guy told him which bed was his for the night and left.

Up early the next morning, Rico went toward the office, seeing several people walking ahead of him, he simply followed. On a large table were styrofoam cups, plates, and plastic forks, along with scrambled eggs, cold toast, bacon, orange juice and coffee.

Later Rico went to the desk and ask if he could come back tonight. "Today I look for job, maybe get job soon."

The man at the desk looked him over, Rico thought he was going to throw him out, finally said, "You are permitted to stay here for one week, after that we evaluate you, sometimes you may stay longer."

"I kitchen worker, where restaurant I can ask?"

"Try Ricky's." he said and turned away.

Rico turned to the guy beside him and ask, "Where Ricky's"

The guy gave a quizzical look and did not immediately respond.

Finally, "Do you mean where is Ricky's restaurant?"

"Si"

The man smiled and gave him directions.

Arriving at Rick's, Rico went to the cashier and asked, "I see owner-ask for job. I kitchen worker long time, good worker, very careful."

The cashier directed him to the office.

The man there said, "Can I help you"

"Rico kitchen worker, very good worker, need job." Rico said.

"What kind of kitchen work do you do?" the man asked.

"Rico wash dishes, keep kitchen clean, sometime take plates from tables after people eat. I work very good for you."

"Do you have a picture I.D., health card and social security card?"

"Si, I work long time in kitchen."

"When would you want to start?" the man asked.

"I start now or soon… Rico need job bad."

"I'll have the lady take your application and over to the clinic and have them test your blood. If it's good you can come to work tonight a 6:00 o'clock; we close at 12:00. You'll have to stay and help clean up everything. That'll usually take an hour, or sometimes a little longer. You'll be paid for eight hours."

"I need place, I have not much money. Where I go?" Rico asked.

"Where did you stay last night?" The man asked

"I stay at mission"

"Maybe you should continue to stay there for a day or two. My name is Ray Grant, the employees call me Mr. Ray. I'm the late shift manager."

"My name Rico Gonzales, you say, 'Hey Rico.' Ray smiled.

14

"**P**atty, do you think Cleo is cleaned up enough to have dinner with us?" Jeb asked facetiously.

"Sure!" she said, "You can introduce him to your friends as your cousin from back East, or maybe your great uncle."

Tony was not mentioned.

The Clancys were pleased by Cleo's table etiquette. The conversation was casual and to Patty's amazement, very pleasant. It was when the bus boy came to clear the table that a drastic change occurred. It was obvious Rico did not recognize Cleo, but Cleo immediately recognized Rico.

Jeb and Patty noticed the change in Cleo and were fearful that something he had eaten was making him sick.

"Are you alright?!" Jeb said in an alarming tone, "Is it something you ate?!"

"No! No! I'm alright, I thought I recognized the busboy." Cleo failed to convince anyone and was extremely quiet the rest of the evening. The incident wasn't mentioned again.

Cleo wondered if his world was about to collapse again. *What on earth does all this mean? Have I been found out—what kind of trouble is brewing? What will this mean to the Clancys; the ones that dragged*

me from the gutter only to learn I haven't been altogether truthful.
Should I make my self known to Rico? One thing for sure, things have
taken a turn and which way they're going is not clear. Jeb has to be told
of the valises; he has to be told of all that's transpired.

The Next morning Jeb picked up Cleo for work and could tell
he was still very disturbed but didn't mention it. When they arrived
at the yard, Cleo unlocked and opened the gate to the entrance and
followed Jeb to the office.

Once inside, Cleo said, "Jeb, I'm about to reveal something
I should have done a long time ago. Perhaps, when I'm finished,
everything we've built on for these few days may fall apart. Let me
tell the complete story.

Cleo began, slowly and deliberately and told the story of the two
murders and how he happened to come to St Ann and eventually
to Jeb's place.

After a long pause with head drooped, Cleo , in a totally subdued
voice, said, "Tonight, I saw the the young man who had befriended
me; he now works at Ricky's. I don't know what that means except
that someone has located me. There is a part of the story I'm not
ready to reveal. I never intended to personally benefit from these
items. However, the longer they remain in my custody, the more
complex this thing becomes."

Looking straight at Jeb, Cleo said, "I don't want to get you
involved in something that would put you at risk, or jeopardize our
friendship. When I came here, I was like a person in the middle of an
ocean, with no means of survival, when along came the Clancy's and
threw me a lifeline, without which, I'm right back in that ocean.'

Pausing for a moment to calm his uneasiness, Cleo continued,

"However; make no mistake, there are people who are looking for those bags, and I believe that in time they'll put together information sufficient to locate me and will do whatever is necessary to get their hands on the bags. My task seems to be to find them before they find me. I believe the kid is vital to learning who they are. Something tells me that I'm the reason he's here.

Jeb was silent for the longest time. Finally, he said, "For the second time, my first impulse is to tell you *to get lost*. But, there's something about you that intrigues me; I feel compelled to help you. Besides, that's the most unbelievable story I've ever heard-- so unbelievable, in fact, it must be true. Again, I ask you, what are your plans?"

"If my suspicions are accurate, I'm being tailed. I can't prove that, but the fact the kid showed up here indicates someone knows I'm here." Cleo said.

"What make you so sure?" Jeb asked dubiously.

Tilting his head slightly, Cleo continued, "O.K.—No one in Marmelle, not even the kid, knows my name: no one knows of my background, no one knows which way I went from the scene, yet the only person with whom I've had anything like an association, shows up in a town in which I had no original idea of staying. Now, that could be a coincidence, but caution is so vital for safety reasons, I believe it's prudent to proceed on that theory."

Jeb sat forward in his chair, "You said there is a part of the story which you're not prepared to reveal. I assume it has something to do with the location of the bags."

Cleo just looked and said nothing.

"If that's true, I'm not interested in their location so long as it's not on my property."

Cleo raised up in his chair, visibly surprised, "Jeb! I can assure you, they are not on your property; I would never involve you in that way."

Moments passed, Cleo continued, "There is a way in which I would appreciate your input. These are some things to be considered: first, we need to learn as much as we can from the kid, such as, who's been talking to him, who's been asking question and the nature of the questions. Answers to these should give us some direction."

Both men grew silent. Finally, Cleo continued, "At some point we have to bring in the authorities, but I'd like to postpone that until I can learn as much as I can of who's involved. I'd like to get to the other side of this thing alive and well."

"What exactly, do you want to do with the bags?" Jeb asked.

"Well eventually, I want to get it into the hands of the authorities. If it were just money, it could be given to some charity, recovery center, hospital, scholarship or any number of good causes. The drugs are altogether something else. For that reason, the authorities have to be the ones to handle both the money and the drugs."

Both Jeb and Cleo sat silently considering what to do next.

15

Psychic Jim sent a text to Bas: *"The kid has arrived but no contact with the tramp yet; the two will likely get together soon-- no contact with the merchandise. Await further advice."*

Bas gave Lucky a call, "Meet at the shop - 8:00 O'clock."

Lucky, still in his African American disguise, arrived first; ten minutes later Bas came.

"The kid is now working at Ricky's" he said. "There hasn't been contact between the kid and the tramp as yet. However, it now appears they are in this thing together."

"Is it time for the Beast to pay the tramp a visit?" Bas asked. "He ran once, what's to keep him from doing it again? If he does, next time we might not be so lucky."

"If the Beast isn't successful, what's to keep the tramp from running?" Lucky asked. "I think we should give it a little more time and keep an eye on him *and* the kid. At some point, one of them is going to check on the goods. It seems to me, that's the only way we have of finding them. So far, we don't have a clue as to their location! As far as we know, the tramp could have stashed them anywhere. What's more, we don't know who else knows of their whereabouts; we don't know if he has revealed anything to his boss; the entire place where he works is a potential hiding place."

"What if we gave the tramp a suspicion he's being watched?" Bas asked. "It might give him cause to check on the bags,—if he still has them."

Lucky, a little agitated, said " On the other hand, if he has someone else helping besides the kid, that person might leave with the goods."

Pausing, both men silently pondered. "Leave the tail on, make every effort not to blow the cover," Lucky said as he indicated the meeting was adjourned.

Bas sent a text to the Phychic: *No change in plan; keep tabs, careful not to be found out.*

16

They closed the yard at five 0'clock, Tony rode away on his bike, and Jeb drove Cleo to the boarding house. As soon as Jeb left, Cleo made his way to the mission. He inquired at the desk for Rico and was given his room number.

When he knocked on the door Rico answered and said, "I find job and will go soon."

"I'm not here concerning your stay, may I come in please?" Cleo said. Rico became nervous but didn't reply right away. He finally opened the door just enough to see Cleo.

"Rico, I'm not here to give you trouble; I'm here as your friend. We have some things to talk about."

Cleo paused for a moment to see if Rico recognized him; it was obvious he did not.

Cleo continued, "I'm the tramp you so graciously fed when you worked for Black Angus."

"You no look same, maybe you come to hurt Rico."

"NO! NO! I didn't come to hurt you! Did you receive a card from someone who said, *From a friend who will never forget—thank for the lift Mi Amigo?*"

Rico nodded.

"I'm that friend."

Rico smiled and with a sigh of relief said, "Rico scared; bad man say he will hurt Rico bad if he tell and policeman say I must tell. I don' know if I tell --if I don' tell. Rico scared and leave town. I have job Ricky's."

"Yes I know, I had dinner there a few nights ago and recognized you. I too, have some concerns for my safety. I was beneath the garbage rack the night the two men were killed. I saw it happen. I saw the bags and took them and ran. I hope to trap the people who are looking for me and the bags. I'm going to need you to help me. I won't ask you to do anything which might endanger you. What I want you to do is tell me all that has happened to you since that night. I need to know who asked you questions and what the questions were about."

Rico turned to get his apron and said,"Friend, Rico must go work. I don' work Saturday, maybe we talk then?"

The two shook hands and Cleo left. Up the street a half block, a car pulled away from the curb and disappeared. Something about it sparked a concern for Cleo. Had he seen it before and maybe more than once? *Don't get paranoid, Cleo, there are thousands of cars,* he said to himself.

Jim, the Psychic, beeped the manager, *"The Tramp made contact with the kid. Meeting was brief. Perhaps something's developing."*

The next morning as they were having coffee, Tony left the office not wanting to be in Cleo's presence.

Cleo said, " Last night I visited the Latino kid and made myself known. He's very scared; someone has put the fear of God in him. He was about to go to work when I arrived, so our meeting was brief. He has agreed to meet me Saturday to bring me up to date about what's happened to him."

Cleo paused briefly, "As I was leaving the kid's place, I noticed a car a short distance from me. The driver pulled away from the curb and disappeared. For some reason, that drew my attention. I don't know if I've seen that car before, but I had that feeling."

With some uncertainty Cleo continued, "Jeb, I'd like to have your permission to come to the yard Saturday. I have a plan that I believe will reveal once and for all that I've been found and if I have a tail.

I'd like to enter the yard at the gate but leave another way. With your permission, I'd like to take the kid with me and see what happens."

"I'll do better than that!" Jeb said, "I'll get in the upper level of the warehouse across the street where I can observe everything around us.

If you have a tail, I'll see him."

"The kid and I will walk to the yard, that'll give you time to get to the warehouse and positioned; also, while the tail is on us, you shouldn't be noticed." Cleo said as he headed to the yard to work.

"Cleo," Jeb said, "I'm sure you've seen it, but in case you haven't, there's a hole torn in the fence on the north west corner, over by the crushed cars. The forklift operator let one of the old cars get into it; we just haven't gotten around to repairing it. The hole is big enough for a person to crawl through. I think you ought to stay out of sight for at least an hour and two would be better. If there *is* a tail, he'll wait to follow you. It's just a matter of which of you out waits the other. The bushes are thick outside the fence, walk west and you'll come to 8th Street. Stay hidden and wait until you see me coming; if I keep going, that means it's not yet safe. Wait 'til I stop and toot, then come get in the car and lay low until we're away from this area."

"Thanks Jeb!" Cleo said, stepping back to shake Jeb's hand.

Saturday morning Cleo was up early, ate his breakfast and went to the mission to meet Rico. Rico was just finishing his breakfast when Cleo arrived and the two went to Rico's room. Cleo brought Rico up to date on the plan for the day. He told him of seeing the car and what he thought it meant. Rico seemed to get upset. He then told Cleo of the threat the goon had made and said he thought they might be there after him. He told Cleo of thinking he recognized the voice of the person making the threat but could not place it.

During the twenty minute walk to the yard, Cleo asked, "Why did you happen to come to this town?"

"I don' know where to go, what town to go, I just show the bus man this card and tell him I go there."

"How did he know from what I wrote on the card that it came from this town…?" As an answer to his own question, "The post mark of course!"

"Do you know if anyone else might have seen this card?" he continued.

"Si! I think boss man at Angus house see it. Mr. Policeman want to see it but I leave before he see it."

"Did anyone else ask to see it?" Cleo asked.

"No—No ask to see but boss man ask who it from. I spill tray and break glass, I cut finger and must leave because of blood. I don' know who see card after I left."

They finally arrived at the yard, Cleo unlocked the gate and looked around as though he was making sure no one was watching as they went inside. He cautiously looked toward the warehouse and got the salute. After entering the yard, he locked the gate and they proceeded to the northwest side. Just as Jeb had said, there was the hole in the fence. Now, the wait began. Beyond the fence was an undeveloped area with small bushes, weeds and grass, providing cover for the kid and Cleo when it came time to leave the yard.

17

Chief Browning drove to the Angus to look at Rico's card. Bas told him the kid had drawn his pay and left and didn't say where he was going.

"Do you have reason to suspect someone other than the police have had contact with him?" The Chief asked, watching the expression on the face of the manager.

"I've not personally seen such a one." Bas answered. The Chief thought he saw a small twitch on his face.

"Does the kid seemed unsettled; is the quality of his work the same?" the Chief asked, again watching Bas closely; again he seemed uncomfortable.

"I can't say there is a noticeable difference," Bas said, trying desperately to be convincing.

As the chief rose to leave the restaurant, he extended his hand and said, "If you hear from the kid, please give me a call, we have some new leads, and he is key to their development."

This time Bas attempted to clear a dry throat, "I'll be glad to." he said.

The Chief phoned headquarters from his car and asked for Watson,

"Can you come down to my office in about fifteen minutes?"

"Sure! I'll be right there." Watson assured him.

The two took their seats and Watson asked, "What's up, Chief?"

"I need a man to keep tabs on an individual that I believe is into this murder case, up to his eyeballs. This is just a theory you understand, I have no hard evidence. I asked the owner to bring the kid who worked at the restaurant to my office, which he did. The kid told me of a card he had received from someone who didn't sign it nor give any evidence from whence it came. When I asked him if he still had the card, he said he did but didn't have it with him. I asked if I could come and look at it and he readily agreed. He and the manager left my office and the kid hasn't been seen since. I went to the restaurant to look at the card, only to discover he had left town."

"Do you think they've harmed the kid?" Watson asked.

"I doubt that," the Chief answered, "but they might have strongly suggested that he leave this area, if you know what I mean."

"What is it you want me to do?" Watson asked, "do you want twenty four hour surveillance on this guy?"

"Yes, for a couple of days. If my suspicions are accurate, we'll know something by then; if not, I'll have misread the guy," Browning said, "If you can spare a couple of men, I'd certainly appreciate it."

"What are we looking for?" Watson asked.

"If he is in on something, I suspect he would have his contacts outside the business. Therefore, I'd pay particular attention to trips he made outside. However; sometimes there might be people in the restaurant who weren't there to eat. In that case, we'd need to keep tabs on those people as well. Keep me posted."

The two men rose, shook hands and Watson left. Watson called two of his best undercover cops, referred to as Shrimp and Curly, filled them in and told them to report any unusual behavior of this guy.

18

Finally, back at the salvage yard, the all clear 'beep, beep' came from Jeb's car. Cleo and Rico quickly made their way to the car, climbed in and hid themselves from the outside.

Jeb said, "Cleo, describe the suspicious car you saw."

"I was quite a ways from it, but it appeared to be an older, medium sized car; possibly a light blue," Cleo said.

Jeb said, "You have a tail. Such a car appeared across the track, positioned himself so as to see you enter the yard. He stayed for about an hour, then drove up and down the street a couple of times and eventually left. I suspect he's still looking for you."

"Now that we're pretty sure I have a tail, we can use that to our advantage," Cleo said.

" I'm a little concerned for your safety now," Jeb said, "It won't be long now before they make some kind of move. I think you'll be in serious danger when that occurs."

With a concerned look Cleo said, "If you're right, Rico may be in danger as well."

"Absolutely!" Jeb said.

Realizing the time had come to share everything with Jeb, Cleo said, "Rico has told me of his abduction and questioning about the night of the murders. They kept his head covered from the time he was abducted until they took him back to his work and were gone. He thinks he recognized one of the voices but can't remember where he'd heard it. They used some very persuasive methods of getting the answers to their questions, and threatened even greater punishment if he told of their taking him. The Chief of Police in Marmelle called Rico in a couple of times and questioned him. Finally he told of his abduction and subsequent threat. His fear, both of the police and the thugs, caused him to leave town. The reason he came here, not knowing where to go, he just showed the card he had gotten from me to the ticket agent. The agent read the name of the town on the postmark."

After a long pause, as both men seemed to be in deep thought, Jeb said, "I think it may be time to go to the Chief and get the professionals in on this. What do you think?"

Pausing to consider the proposal, Cleo said, "I think I agree. However; when we do this, we lose control of the situation. The question is, are we ready to do that?" As if to question his own decision, Cleo said, "If we wait until they come for me--and they will come for me— it's then we learn who's behind this. Since no one but me knows where the goods are, it's not likely they'll deal me serious injury until they have them. Even so…if and when they find a way to get their hands on those bags, my life will be in jeopardy. We *must* be in control when that critical moment comes."

Bas' beeper startled him, supposing it was from the Phychic, he hastily walked to his office.

The message read: *'I may have been made. The tramp and the kid went to the salvage yard Saturday morning, a day the business is usually closed. They didn't leave the way they went in. Intentional or not, they gave me the slip. Await instructions.'*

Because of the time of day, a phone call wouldn't be wise. So, Bas texted Lucky: *Phychic has been made; suggest we move.*

Shortly a return message came, *'8 o'clock @ the shop.'*

Bas arrived at 8 o'clock sharp; Lucky was waiting.

"The Phychic thinks he's been made, so what suggestions do you have?" Bas asked.

"Does he believe the goods are stashed in the salvage yard?" asked Phychic.

"That wasn't mentioned. What are your thoughts on that?" Bas asked.

"Well, we can't be certain. If going to the yard on Saturday was a ploy, the goods are probably not there; on the other hand, if it was not a ploy, the goods are likely there or nearby."

Both men were silent for several moments, finally *Physic* said, "It's time for plan "B".

19

Meanwhile, Curly, one of Watson's detectives, called him and said, "I think I might have something for you."

Watson said, "Meet me at the Chief's office."

Watson and Curly arrived at Chief Browning's office within the hour. The receptionist notified the Chief of their arrival, and they were ushered into his office.

"Curly may have something," Watson said.

"OK. Let's have it." said the Chief.

"About 8 o'clock tonight, the manager of the steak house made a trip to a warehouse, one I believe he uses for storage. He took nothing into the building and brought nothing out. He entered the building and stayed for a relatively short time, then left. That would not be so suspicious except ten minutes later another individual left the same building. I was quite a ways away and was unable to get a good look at him," Curly said.

"We may be close to something," the chief said. "Does anyone know the whereabouts of the kid? Is there a way we can get in touch with him?"

"If indeed, he left town, and since he has no car, he just might have left by bus." Watson said, "Do you think the ticket agent would remember if the kid bought a ticket and would he give us that information?"

"That's a great idea Watson," the chief said, "There's one way to find out." He pushed the intercom and said to his receptionist, "Beth, get me the bus station."

"Right Chief, are you finally leaving town?" she asked, chuckling.

"You're not that lucky, girl."

Almost before the joshing was complete, Beth said, "The ticket agent is on the line.

"The Chief described Rico to the agent and asked if he remembered anyone fitting that description.

"Well, as a matter of fact I do. This young Latino came here and acted like he didn't know where he wanted to go. He handed me an envelope and said, 'I go here.' I looked at the envelope and back at him, not knowing what he meant. Finally he pointed to the postmark which read St. Ann. When I asked if he was going one way or round trip he didn't understand the question, and I asked if he was coming back or staying. He said, 'I no come back.'"

With no hope of getting a yes, the Chief asked, "I don't suppose you happened to see the content of the envelope?"

"I'm sorry, I did not." The agent said.

"Thank you, I appreciate your help."

The Chief hung up and turned to Watson, "The agent remembers the kid. He bought a ticket to St Ann. Do you make anything from that?"

Watson shook his head and said, "Well there are many inferences one might draw from the information we have."

"Watson, does it seem logical to you that this card came from the tramp?"

"Yes sir, it does." Watson said. "If he was once in St Ann, he just might still be there"

"Do you think the kid and the tramp arranged to meet in St Ann?" The chief asked. Watson simply shook his head.

"I believe we should proceed on the assumption the tramp took whatever the victims had?" the chief said.

"I can think of no better scenario," Watson said. "I believe it's imperative we talk to the tramp."

Seemingly in deep thought, the Chief said, "If we are to believe the kid, the tramp has what we need to move this investigation along. Our immediate problem is finding him. St. Ann is not that big; if someone with no more means of support than this tramp is throwing lots of money around, it's certain he would be noticed."

"We seem to be evading the suggestion we're both considering," Watson said smiling.

"Do you have a good man you can send down there for a couple of days to look around," the Chief asked.

"Yes sir." Watson assured him.

Standing, signaling the close of the meeting, the Chief said, "Tell you what: pick your man, bring him to my office and let's fill him in on what we know and send him down there."

The two shook hands and Watson left the office.

Watson returned to his office and paged his receptionist, "Wanda, get me C.I.D."

Only moments later, Wanda said, "Reynolds with C. I. D. is on the line."

"Reynolds, I need one of your best men for an out of town assignment," Watson said, "Who've you got?"

"Give me a couple of hours to find a man and I'll call you." Reynolds answered.

Soon Reynolds called, "I have your man, when would you like to see us?"

"Right away, at your convenience. Meet us at the Chief's office"

The three men arrived, "Come in fellas, have a seat," said the Chief.

"This is detective Paul Snider." Reynolds said.

Snider offered his hand and said, "I'm sure you don't know me, but I've heard so much about you, and may I say I greatly admire you; it's nice to finally meet you."

"Okay Snider, here's where we are. You're aware of the double murders some time ago?"

Snider nodded.

"It looks as if the two men killed each other. It's a strange case and we're still uncertain of some things. We're assuming it's a drug deal gone bad, but we've found no evidence of drugs or money. Prior to the killings, there was a tramp that came to the back of the restaurant at night for food, provided by a young Latino who worked there. The tramp hasn't been seen since the event. We questioned the kid a few times, but it didn't yield much. He has since left town. We have good reason to believe he is in St. Ann, a town about two hundred miles south."

"I've been there." Snider interjected.

The Chief, somewhat taken aback by Snider's interruption, continued, "Furthermore, the same evidence leads us to believe the tramp is also there. We believe he's the key to the solution of this case. What we want you to do is go to St Ann, find this guy, if he's there, find where he's staying, and if he has gotten a job. Find out anything that would tend to shed light on what happened that night. You know we have no authority in that town, so be discreet. Report as soon as you have something. Have the office issue you a credit card; keep all receipts"

"Absolutely sir." Snider said.

20

The restaurant was very crowded and it was difficult for Rico to keep up. As he cleared the table, three men, a couple of tables behind him, were visiting and enjoying their dinner.

Suddenly Rico became very upset and ran to the office and told Ray, "Rico sick, must go to room." Before Ray could even ask about him, he was gone.

Rico ran all the way to the boarding house and down to Cleo's room and began pounding frantically on his door.

"What in the world is the matter?!" Cleo asked.

"Man who have voice I think I hear and don' remember?" Rico asked.

"Yes."

"Tonight he come to Ricky's. I hear him talking, he is black man. My

boss at Angus with him, also man I dunno. I think he come here to kill Rico!"

Cleo put his hand on his shoulders and said, "Rico! Calm down! No one's here to kill you. They're here to see me. They've gotten what they want from you. Remember the day we went to the yard and hid out? Later Jeb told us we were being watched?"

"Si"

"The one you don't know is the guy who was watching us." Cleo said,

"They'll probably make a move soon. We're lucky you recognized this guy, he doesn't know we're on to him yet."

Snider called the office and asked to speak to the chief.

"Chief, Paul Snider is on the line."

"Thanks Beth, put him on."

"Good Morning, Paul, what've you got?"

"Maybe nothing—maybe something. Last night while having dinner at one of the better restaurants, I saw an individual I could swear was the guy who owns the Angus Steak House there. He was with two other sinister individuals. If indeed this was the guy, what would he be doing here?"

Complete silence-- Snider thinking the Chief had hung up, asked, "Are you still there?"

"Yes, I'm here, I'm trying to put two and two together. One thing of which I'm certain, if you haven't located the tramp, keep your eye on these guys—they'll take you to him."

Again the Chief paused, "I'm afraid the tramp's in real danger. If they get to him before the police do, they'll hurt him, maybe worse."

"What do you suggest"? Snider asked.

Once again the Chief took a moment to reflect. "We have a problem. Even if we find him before they do something, we don't know if he has what we're looking for."

21

A short toot on the horn announced the arrival of Jeb to pick up Cleo for work.

"You look rather haggard this morning—anything wrong?" Jeb asked.

Hesitantly Cleo began, "As a matter of fact there is. There are men here from Marmelle looking for me. Rico saw them at Ricky's last night. He recognized his old boss. I have reason to believe they are prepared to move. This is a critical moment. Alone, I won't be able to handle it. At some point they're going to grab me. If I give them what they want, they will dispose of me-- thinking the death of a tramp would mostly go unnoticed. If I refuse to give them the bags, they'll make me very miserable. I'm prepared to endure some of their punishment in order to be credible. When I reveal the location of the goods, I need to have some security."

Jeb, realizing he hadn't even started the engine, said, "Cleo, we have to go to the authorities!"

Cleo, raising his voice, "Which authority? If we go to the local police, they are going to want to go head long into this thing. If this happens, the case against these thugs is going to be greatly diminished. We need to allow them possession of the bags before any arrests are made. If I go to the state police, I lose all control and run the risk of being arrested myself.

I'm sure the investigation of this matter is still ongoing in Marmelle."

Both men grew silent, each deeply engrossed in his own thoughts. Finally Cleo broke the silence, "Jeb, are you acquainted with the police chief here?"

"Well, yes, I know who he is".

"Do you think he might cooperate with our plan?'

Jeb jerked his head toward Cleo, "What plan?"

"I mean, if we had a plan that would require his participation without involving the entire police force-- sort of acting alone."

"What are you getting at?" Jeb said, a little impatient.

Cleo, anxious to get things in motion, said, "The people who are here looking for me are from Marmelle; the authorities there will be more interested in these guys because the crime was committed there. Here's the scenario: if we're going to catch them with the goods, at some point, I have to take them to it. Before I'm willing to expose myself, I want protection. I'm convinced, without it, I'm history. Just how that protection can be provided is something yet to be arranged."

A momentary pause and Cleo continued, "If we don't involve the local police in some way, there's going to be a big to do over that. However, if the local chief is included, that should dispel that riff. At the point of making arrests, we'll need the help of his entire force."

As if he had reached a final decision Cleo asked, "Do you think the chief would come to your office and talk to us?"

Jeb thought for a moment, "Well, let's find out."

Jeb drove hurriedly to the office, Tony was waiting with the gate open,

"Tony, take the day off, I have some things to take care of. You'll be paid for the day." Tony turned to Cleo with a look of disdain, then climbed on his bike and rode away.

Jeb and Cleo entered the yard and into the office. Jeb picked up the phone and dialed the police station. "Is Chief Jordan in?"

"Yes Sir, may I ask who's calling?"

"Jeb Clancy."

"One moment please."

Bill Jordan picked up his receiver and said, "Good morning Jeb, how can I help you?

"I need to talk to you away from your office. I wonder if you would take a few minutes and come to my place?"

"Sure, I don't have anything on the early agenda—could we do it now?" Jordan asked.

"That would be wonderful; I'll have the coffee on." Jeb promised.

Bill arrived a few minutes later and Jeb met him at the gate.

In a quiet voice, Jeb whispered, "Bill, we are being watched; please follow my lead." Bewildered, Bill just stood looking, wondering what to do next.

Jeb walked out the gate and pointing down the fence line and in a muted voice, said, "I'm pretending I've asked you here for something to do with my business." He elaborately waved his arms up and down as to question something about the fence. Turning to Bill and motioning toward the office, "I think we can go inside now." All the way into the office Jeb would stop, turn toward the fence and motion with his hands.

Finally inside the office Bill had had all he wanted. "Jeb, what on earth is the matter with you?! Are you on something?"

"Bill, please have a seat. You may be more bewildered after you hear our story. There is a fella whom I have had working for me for a few weeks. I have come to have total confidence in his work as well as his honesty. I have to warn you, what you are about to hear will challenge your imagination."

"Let me introduce you: "Bill, this Cleo Hertzwitz," turning to Cleo, "Bill Jordan." The two men shook hands.

"Cleo, maybe you should start at the beginning."

Cleo went through the entire story: his downfall, the feeding by the Latino, the murders, his flight to St Ann and now being confident of his imminent abduction and possible harm.

For several moments there was complete silence, the three men taking turns looking at each other.

Finally Jordan said, "Well, now that you have my attention, please continue."

"I caught a slow moving train, rode it to St. Ann, not intentionally of course, that just happened to be where the train stopped. I have hidden the bags; they're safe. I'm the only one who knows where they are. I have my reasons for keeping their location a secret. One of those reasons, I think it will help nail the thugs that are after me, and the guys to whom the bags were to be delivered."

Jordan, getting a little uncomfortable with all this, said, "So far, you've told me of seeing two men kill each other and of your taking two bags and running; you don't choose to tell what you've done with them and haven't hinted at what you expect me to do."

"I'm sorry, Sir! I don't mean to be vague; it's just that I know these guys will come for me very soon, and when they do, I want to be prepared to give them what they want but make sure I'm protected at the same time. I'm not looking to become morgue fodder. I believe the authorities can provide both that protection and the arrest of these guys at the same time with the goods in their hands."

The men sat silent for several minutes, each one with his own thoughts.

Finally Jordan said, "I'm not sure I can help you. You see, the crime you've described wasn't committed in my jurisdiction. I can't give you police protection without cause. As serious as this situation is for you, the truth is, I have no legal authority to become involved. My suggestion is for you to go to Marmelle and talk to the chief there. We'll certainly assist in any way we can here, but the initiative has to be with him."

"Well, I feel sure I would not arrive safely if I try that on my own." Cleo said.

Jordan, after mulling over what had been said, "Here's what I'll do for you if you'd like; I'll call the chief there and ask him if he has an interest in you. If he does, we can go from there."

Jeb looked at Cleo, "What do you think of that idea?"

"I think if we do that, I want to talk to him personally, after you've explained this situation. Is that going to be a problem?"

"Not for me, but I don't know about him, we'll have to handle this his way," Jordan said.

"No one there knows my name or who I am!" Cleo said. "When you talk to him, I think you may have to explain my homeless condition at that time. I think he'll remember me."

"When would you like to contact Marmelle?" Jordan asked.

"Are you prepared to talk to them?" Cleo asked.

"Yes." Jordan nodded.

"Because I'm being watched, I don't need to be seen with the police chief." Cleo continued, "Could you place the call from here?"

Jeb looked at Jordan; Jordan looked at Jeb. Finally Jeb motioned toward the telephone. Jordan picked up the phone, "Marmelle please." A brief pause, "Police department please." Another pause... "Thank you." Jordan placed the call.

"Hello, this is Chief of Police Bill Jordan in St. Ann. I'd like to speak to your chief."

Cheerfully as usual Beth said, "Chief, A Bill Jordan, chief of police in St. Ann is on line one."

"Thanks Beth."

"This is Chuck Browning, how can I help you?"

"Hello Chief, I have someone here you may be interested in. He tells me of a rather unusual event which took place in your town some time ago involving a double killing. If what he says is true, he may be in jeopardy. He would like to talk to you. Before he does, let me assure you of our cooperation and assistance in this matter if we are needed."

Jordan handed Cleo the phone, "He definitely has an interest in you."

"Hello Chief, you don't know me by name, but you will by description. I'm the old guy who often came to the alley where the two men were killed. It just so happens I was witness to those killings."

"Can you describe the nature of the killings?" the Chief asked, making sure this was not some kind of hoax.

"Yes Sir!" Cleo said, "One of the men stabbed the other and the stabbed man shot the other."

"How is it you were in proximity of this scene?" the chief asked.

Cleo answered without hesitation, "At night I often went to the rear of that restaurant looking for food. On this night, as I was about to reach the area the two cars entered the alley. Not wanting to be found, I crawled under the garbage rack. After the killings, I took two valises and caught a train to St. Ann. Although I have no personal interest in their contents, I've hidden the bags. I'm interested in catching the ones who were to benefit from them."

"I have a man in St. Ann looking for you, could it be that man is the one following you?" The chief asked.

"No," Cleo answered, "there are three men in this group. Rico, a young Latino lad, worked for the Angus restaurant in your town. Now he has a job at a restaurant here. Three men came into that restaurant; one he recognized as the owner of the Angus. This young man is extremely afraid of these men."

After a brief pause, Cleo continued, "One night as Rico was on his way to work at the Angus, some guy grabbed him and drove him to a place where he was brought before another man. They placed a device around his ankle and began to question him. When his answers didn't suit them, they gave him a strong electrical shock. They did this numerous times. Eventually, after threatening him with severe harm if he told of the abduction, they released him. Rico recognized the voice of one of the threesome as the one who had questioned him. He has no idea who the third man is. It is these three men who are interested in me and the missing items."

"Why is it that you won't reveal the whereabouts of these bags?" Chief Browning asked.

Cleo answered, "I assure you sir I have no other motive than to make sure these guys are caught. If I reveal the bags' whereabouts, it makes it possible for that information to fall into the wrong hands. If something goes wrong before these men are apprehended, my life will be in real jeporady. When we have accomplished our mission, believe me! I will gladly reveal everything I know about this whole matter."

"Let me talk to Jordan," Browning said. Reluctantly, Cleo offered Jordan the phone.

"This is Jordan."

"What's your take on this guy?" he asked.

"He is either genuine or the best actor I've seen. He appears to be greatly concerned for his safety." Jordan said.

"How are we going to proceed if we don't know the people that are after him? It's possible the owner of the Angus is there. I have had him under surveillance and have observed some suspicious activity, but he has not been around for a few days. Furthermore, we don't know for sure what this guy has or where it is." Browning said.

Cleo, getting the attention of Jordan, said, "Before you hang up, I want to talk to the Chief."

Jordan handed Cleo the phone, "Hello again Chief, I'd like to ask a favor of you; would you have your man from Marmelle get in touch with me?"

There was silence.

Finally, Cleo said,"I want to go over a plan for getting these guys. If my plan is a good one, we will need the cooperation of the police here. After talking with your man and then getting the approval of the police here as well as those of you in Marmelle, I'm prepared to reveal what I know as well as where the valises are."

"This is highly unusual and also appears to be dangerous; ordinary citizens are rarely used in police work. However, I will have Paul Snider contact you. Under no circumstance are you to involve any police force until everyone knows the facts of this case and what to expect." Browning warned.

"I understand Sir and I give you my word, the police will have full knowledge of what will most surely happen and will have absolute control of the event." assured Cleo, "It's imperative that Snider contact me at the office to set up a place for our meeting. I'm being watched and every effort must be taken to prevent those who are on to me from learning of our plot. Our success depends on secrecy." added Cleo.

22

In order to avoid suspicion, Bas, Lucky, and Beast stayed in separate motels, but met at Ricky's for breakfast.

Lucky, who seemed to be the ring leader, said, "We have to get our hands on this guy soon, this has gone on far too long. Let's hear some ideas."

"We can hardly walk into the place of business and take him," Bas said.

"That wouldn't bother me!" chimed in the Beast.

"What about the kid who works at the junk yard with the tramp?" Bas asked.

"I reckon I never knew a kid who couldn't use a hundred dollars," Beast added.

"Can we talk to him without being watched?" Lucky asked.

"He rides a bicycle to work, I can follow him home and feel him out if you'd like." Bas volunteered.

"It's important to find out how he feels about this tramp." Lucky said.

"Call me around nine o'clock tonight and I'll let you know what I find"

Bas said.

At five O'clock, Tony hopped on his bike and headed for home. Bas stayed a great distance behind, but as Tony pulled into a driveway, he hurried to catch up.

Rolling down the window he said, "Could I ask you a question please?"

Tony walked up to the car and asked, "What's the question?"

"Do you work for Jeb Clancy?"

"Yeah,what about it?"

"There's another guy who works there as well, right?"

"Yeah,what about him?"

"Do you know his name?"

"Yeah, it's Cleo Hertzwitz." Tony said scornfully.

"What's your opinion of him, if you don't mind my asking?" Bas asked.

"I think he's a jerk."

Bas said, "I think he has something that belongs to me. I wonder if you'd like to help me find out for sure? It'll be worth a hundred dollars to you."

"What do I have to do?" the kid asked.

"Just watch what he does and where he goes. If he goes to a certain place in the yard for no apparent reason, or if he goes outside somewhere away from the business at any time-things like that."

"Sure! I'll be glad to. How can I get in touch with you?" the kid asked.

"Here's my number. They call me Bas, call me any time. In fact, if he leaves the area for any reason, I want you to call me immediately and let me

know." Bas said, shook the kid's hand and drove away.

23

It was 4:30 and things were winding down at the yard.

Reluctantly, Cleo said, "Jeb before we go home I'd like to check on something."

"Can I help you with anything?" Jeb asked.

"Oh no! It'll only take a few minutes; I'll be back by 5."

"Sure. Go ahead." Jeb said, but thought it unusual.

Cleo left the yard, acting as though he was making sure no one was watching. He covered the 300 yards to the creek at a brisk pace, all the while keeping an eye out for trouble. The valises had not been disturbed; nothing seemed to have been bothered. He wondered if it was time to partially uncover them. Remembering his promise to Chief Browning, he decided against it.

Cleo felt sure this trip to the creek would not go unnoticed. He felt that he had to get in touch with Paul Snider.

Arriving back at the office just as everyone was closing up. Tony gave Cleo a quizzical look but said nothing.

"That's strange," Cleo thought, then passed it off as being paranoid.

Just as everyone was ready to walk out of the office, the phone rang and Cleo picked up the receiver, "I'd like to speak with a Cleo Hertwitz please."

"This is he. How can I help you?"

"This is Paul Snider, my boss tells me I'm to meet with you. Are you free tonight?" Paul asked.

"Yes, as a matter of fact I am. If you'll give me a number, I'll give you a call in a few minutes. We are about to close up and go home."

"That'll be fine." and gave Cleo the number and hung up.

Again, Tony seemed to hang on every word.

Cleo called Jeb aside and said, "Would you hang around a few minutes after Tony leaves?"

"Sure! What's up?"

"Tonight I'm meeting with Paul Snider, the guy from Marmelle, I'm going to set a trap, myself being the bait. We can only hope it works."

Neither spoke for a moment, finally Cleo continued, "I'm prepared to reveal all I know pertaining to this situation. Because you've been the super friend to me, I want you to know what I know and what I'm going to do."

A concerned look came over Jeb's face, "Surely you are not going into this thing alone?"

"Of course not. After I talk with Paul tonight, I expect to have him alert the police here."

"What can I do?" Jeb asked

"Stay at the yard, or nearby. I'm not sure how many will be involved in the abduction. When I first got off the boxcar from Marmelle, I was near the creek behind the yard. I buried one of the two valises beneath the bridge, the other one is top side. I'm not sure what's in them, as I never opened them. I suspect there is a rather large sum of money in one and drugs in the other."

✳

Bas' phone rang, Tony asked to speak to him."Go ahead."

"Well, the guy left the work area today at 4:30 and was gone for about thirty minutes. I don't know where he went but appeared to be going toward the railroad."

" Has he done this before?" Bas asked.

"I haven't noticed it if he has." Tony said. "When do I get my $100.00?"

"In due time. When I'm able to get in touch with him and ask some questions I'll give you the money." Bas promised.

24

Cleo dialed Paul Snider's number. "Paul, this is Cleo. I'm sorry if I seemed brief before; I had someone near whom I didn't want to hear our conversation."

"That's no problem," Paul assured him.

Cleo continued, "Paul, it's safer if we talk in your car. I'd like for you to pick me up on 8th Street at 8:30. The street parallels the salvage yard on the west side. As you pull even with the yard, flip your lights, I'll cross the brushy area to your car."

At 8:30 Paul, driving along 8th,, flipped his light and Cleo emerged.

As they pulled away Cleo said, "Here's my plan and I remain open for any suggestion. I believe these guys are waiting for an opportunity to nab me. I realize the risks involved, but I'm O.K. with that if we can nail the goons with the goods in hand." Cleo waited for some sign: approval or disapproval. None came.

"Let's assume I make myself vulnerable; for example, I walk home after eating dinner at Ricky's. We know they are there every night. I believe they'll take the bait."

After yet another a pause, "It seems logical they'll want to get their hands on the missing valises, how they go about it presents the greater risks."

"At what point are the police to get involved?" Paul asked, "And how are we to know where you are?"

"I'll give you that information after we decide if this is how we are to proceed," Cleo said.

"You seem to have all the cards, what is it you would have me do from here?" Paul said.

"I'd like for Chief Jordan to put his men on alert and be ready to move quickly. After the plan is fully set, I'll reveal the location of the valises. It's then I believe everything will happen."

Cleo paused, wondering if Paul was actually interested in this whole thing. "If we can be assured of Chief Jordan's cooperation, this is how I want to proceed: There is a warehouse across the street from the salvage yard with a large upper room. A window in the rear allows a wide view of our area. My boss Jeb will be there. The location of the valises is in proximity to that building." Cleo continued, "They are at separate locations. After the thugs take possession of the first valise and as we proceed to the second, presents the opportunity for the arrests."

Paul seemed to be in deep thought, "I'll get in touch with Chief Jordan and see what his feelings are. I suppose he'll want to relay everything to Chief Browning in Marmelle.

25

At Ricky's, the three men were engaged in serious conversation.

Lucky leaned back in his chair and said, "We have everything we're gonna to get. We know the guy we want, we know who he is, we know where he works and we know where he lives. Taking him captive constitutes some risk," Lucky continued, "However, it has to be done. The longer we put it off, the greater the chances become that we'll never be able to reclaim what belongs to us."

After a pause, Lucky continued, "It's not a good idea to go where he lives; we have to nail him before he arrives. It's pretty obvious he's on to us."

Not to be outdone, Beast chimed in, "We can't afford to botch this thing! We're going to have ONE---just one chance to pull this off. If we botch it, there's a good chance we'll lose our freedom. I believe, given a little more time, staying a little closer to him, an opportunity will present itself."

"He sometimes has dinner with his boss and his wife." Lucky said, "That could be our best opportunity. Let's watch Ricky's very close and be ready to move quickly when the opportunity arises."

After a period of contemplation, Lucky said, "Bas, you drive. You need to be in the car and ready to move in if we're able to get our hands on him. From there we'll take him to my motel, the

equipment is there. What about the other kid who works there?"
Lucky continued. "He's willing to help us. What are some of your
thoughts?

Bas said, "He doesn't like him and the tramp knows it. Because
of that, it's not going to be easy to arrange something."

"Maybe the kid could ask him to help him with something at
his home," Beast offered.

"That might work," Lucky said. "Bas, can you get in touch with
him again"

"Sure, I have his cell number."

Lucky said, "Call him and set up something."

Bas called Tony. "We want you to arrange for Hertwitz to be
walking alone—maybe toward your house after work. Think you
can arrange it?"

"I want my hundred bucks before I do anymore." Tony said.

"As soon as we have Hertwitz, you get the hundred." Bas said.

"Huh-uh, I want it now or the deal is off." Tony said defiantly.

"I'll meet you at your house shortly after five o'clock." Bas
promised.

Tony and Cleo were helping with a customer. After the customer
left, Tony said, "Look Cleo, we have to work together, it would be a
lot better for both of us if we became friends. I know I haven't been
the most congenial person since you've been here, but I'm ready to
make it up to you. I'd like to buy your dinner. I know you live alone
and I live with my mother. It so happens she's gone to spend a couple
of days with her sister. What do you say?"

"I'd like that." Cleo said.

"Whadda you say? Ricky's at eight—my treat. I'll come by and we can walk to Ricky's together." He added.

As promised, Bas was at Tony's with the hundred dollars.

"We'll be at Ricky's at 8 o'clock. I'm buying his supper—sorta like Judas."

"Good work Tony."

"We'll be walking both ways, do what you have to do." Tony said nonchalantly.

26

Cleo called Snider, "Do you have anything arranged"?

"I've talked to Jordan and he has agreed to alert his men. He has called Marmelle; they are standing by. We don't know exactly what to expect."

"It's going to happen tonight. The kid who works with me has never offered to be friendly; as a matter of fact, he's been downright hostile. Today he offered to buy my dinner. We are to be at Ricky's at 8:00. I'm sure there will be someone nearby to make the grab."

"Where are the police to be situated?" Paul asked.

"Along the railroad beside the salvage yard going north, there's a small creek. One of the valises is buried beneath the bridge on the north side of the creek, the other is buried on the top side of the bridge between the rails.

Cleo paused, waiting for some encouragement-none came.

Finally he contiued, "If this thing goes down as I expect, I'll be accompanied to the location by these three thugs. When I uncover and give them the first valise and after they have it in their hands, the arrests can be made."

Again Cleo paused, hoping for agreement - again nothing.

"The sooner these men are in custody, the healthier I'll be."

Cleo, emphatic now, "There needs to be someone in the vicinity of Ricky's tonight; the progression has to be monitored very closely, careful not to blow the entire operation. These guys will have police scanners, therefore there must be complete radio silence; communication will have to be through cell phones." Cleo warned "the critical point of this thing is when we actually began to uncover the bags. Therefore, everything and everybody must be in place by 8:00."

Benson and Dudley, two plain-clothed cops, were assigned to tail the detail if and when it left the motel.

After hanging up with Snider, Cleo called Jeb and related the information and asked if he could man the warehouse.

"Absolutely!" Jeb said.

"You will probably be the director of this thing once we are on our way to the bags." Cleo said in tone of appreciation. "Get in touch with Jordan, get his cell number and pre-dial it. When you see us coming from the creek, tell Jordan we're ready for them to take them down."

"Consider it done. Cleo! Watch your step, these guys play for keeps, so be careful."

27

Tony and Cleo walked toward the restaurant, the conversation was obviously strained. Tony appeared extremely uncomfortable but managed to hold up his end of the conversation. Small talk about the activity of the day at the yard was the topic. Occasionally, Tony would look behind him. Cleo wondered if the thugs would come before he and Tony had eaten.

It was difficult for Cleo to conceal his feelings but felt like he had.

They approached the hostess, "Two?" she asked. Tony nodded. She led them to a booth and soon the waiter was there taking their orders. When their food arrived, Cleo began to eat but noticed Tony didn't.

"Are you not feeling well?" Cleo asked.

Tony picked up his fork . "Yeah, I feel alright, I'm just not very hungry."

"If you don't feel well, we can go." Cleo offered.

"No, I'm fine." Tony said, with just a tinge of cynicism. Not much was discussed during the rest of the meal.

As soon as Cleo was finished, Tony said, "I'm ready to go as soon as you are."

"Sure." Cleo said.

Tony motioned to the waiter, requested the bill, walked to the cashier, paid, and walked on toward the door. Cleo couldn't help but notice Tony's anxiety.

Once away from the lights of the restaurant, Tony began to be more and more fidgety. It wasn't a long wait. The car pulled alongside of Cleo, two men jumped from the car and grabbed him, roughly shoving him in and then sped away. The two plain-clothed cops were just about to pull away from Ricky's when the abduction occurred. Jordan's cell rang, "This is Benson; the abduction has occurred. The principle has been carried to the "Sleep-Well Motel on 5th.

28

Once inside, Lucky roughly shoved Cleo into a chair, "You've been a real problem for us for quite some time now. You took something that belongs to us, and we're going to ask you tell us where it is. First, we're going to be polite and say please. If we don't get the correct answers, you'll become more and more uncomfortable." *I now know why Rico recognized this voice*, Cleo thought. *African American or whatever... that's Ruis.*

"Mr. Tramp, would you please tell us where the stolen items are?" Lucky asked. Cleo sat quietly, showing no sign of responding. Lucky turned to Beast and nodded. Beast then jerked up Cleo's pant leg and placed the electronic device on his leg. When he finished, he looked at Lucky and nodded.

"Mr. Tramp, we want to know where the stolen items are." Again, Cleo just sat looking at Lucky. This time when Lucky nodded, a bolt of electricity went through Cleo's leg causing him to cry out.

"Mr. Tramp, we're waiting for your answer." Lucky smirked. Cleo said nothing. Lucky nodded. This time the charge lasted much longer, making Cleo realize he had to do something.

"Mr. Tramp, if you fail to answer my question this time, you'll regret it for the rest of your life—which may not be a long time, if you get what I mean. Tell us where it is." Cleo didn't speak right away. When he saw Lucky nod, he hurriedly began to speak.

"I don't have the bags with me. They are at separate locations and I'm the only person on earth who knows where they are." Cleo said, looking confidently into the eyes of Lucky. "Because I was once a tramp, is no indication I'm a fool. I know that as soon as you have what you want, I'm dead. I'm also confident that as long as you don't have them, the chances of my staying alive are greatly improved. I can assure you these bags will never be found unless I reveal their location." Cleo said, pausing long enough for the thugs to think on that.

"Now here's the deal: I haven't opened either of them, consequently I don't know what's in which of them. I'm willing to take you to one of the bags; you can take possession of it. Once you have the bag in your hand, I'm released; nobody goes with me.

Cleo watched his abductor to see if what he was saying was credible.

He continued, "After I'm released, I'll tell you where you can get instructions for retrieving the other.

"How do you propose to tell us if you are not with us?" Beast asked.

"There will be written instructions placed at a place which I'll reveal at the right time." Cleo said.

"Let's move!" Lucky said, "Lead the way Mr. Tramp."

"Just a minute" Cleo said, "I haven't gotten your assurance that you'll follow the plan I've outlined." That said to bolster the thugs' ego and quell any suspicion they might have. Cleo realized they weren't going to follow anyone's plan except their own.

"O.K. You have my word," Lucky said.

"Drive to the salvage yard first," Cleo instructed.

Bas turned to Beast and said, "I told you the stuff was somewhere in that junk yard."

Pulling up to the gate, Lucky asked, "Mr. Tramp, can you open the gate?"

"There's no need for that, the bags aren't in the yard."

"Wait a minute!—are you leading us into a trap?" Lucky asked.

"You either trust me or you don't." Cleo said.

Getting out of the car Cleo said, "Follow me." and began walking toward the creek. 'We'll need a light—anyone bring one?"

"There's a small one in the car," Bas said.

Turning to the dubious thugs Cleo asked, "Are you coming or not?"

Arriving at the creek, Cleo went straight to the rocks covering the valise. A few minutes later he offered it to Lucky. He jerked the valise from Cleo's hand and demanded that Cleo hand over the other one.

"I'll write the directions and pin them on the side of the gate, you'll have to give me ten minutes---------." Cleo said,

"We don't have to give you anything. Our next stop is back at the motel. We have ways of getting those directions, as you'll soon find out."

"But you gave me your word!" Cleo said in a whimpering tone.

"We're not known for keeping our word." Lucky said, releasing a victory laugh.

"Please, if you'll just let me go, I'll take you to the other bag." Cleo was convincing.

"Okay! We have no interest in anything but what's in the bags. Lead the way."

"They're coming up Bill!" informed Jeb, "Wait 'til I say go."

Jeb began to count. "1-,2,-3-,4-,5---15. "Bill, it's in your hands."

In 3 seconds policemen came from every angle yelling, "ON THE GROUND. GET ON THE GROUND!!!!"

Lucky, dropped the bag, grabbed Cleo and put a gun to his head and yelled, "Call off your dogs or this low life gets it in the back of the head!"

"Hold you fire!" Jordan yelled.

"Beast, get the bag and let's get out of here. The tramp goes with us, if any of you cowboys try something heroic, he dies." Lucky smirked.

Beast grabbed the bag and the thugs began their back-peddling toward the car. As they reached the car Lucky said, "Open the back door." They shoved Cleo in car and closed the door.

Benson and Dudley emerged from behind the car, Benson said, "If you turn around with that gun in your hand, you're a dead man. Get on the ground!! Get on the ground—dead or alive, get on the ground, NOW!"

Slowly Lucky dropped the gun and the three hit the ground. Dudley systematically handcuffed the three. Benson yelled, "In custody!" Jordan and the other officers, guns drawn, quickly made their way to the scene.

Cleo emerged from the car, "Jordan, I must say, having Benson and Dudley positioned at the car was a bit of wisdom to say the least. Thanks!"

"All in a day's work" Jordan said.

The three were taken to jail. Jordan took possession of the bag.

Cleo came to Jordan, "The other bag is nearby, I'll get it for you." A few feet from where it all took place, Cleo unearthed the valise.

"I'm not sure what I'm supposed to do with you." Jordan said, "I'm sure Marmelle will have to talk to you. "

Cleo said, "I'm not going anywhere, if Marmelle needs me, I'm prepared to go there."

Back at the office, Jordan dialed Marmelle,

"Police department." The radio lady said.

"Chief Browning please. This is chief Paul Jordan of the St. Ann police department"

"I'm sorry. Chief Browning has gone home for the day. Can someone else help you?"

"Please get in touch with him, have him give me a call right away ; it's very urgent."

"Certainly, sir. Does he have your number?"

"I'm not sure, but I'll be at my headquarters in about fifteen minutes."

Jordan had barely gotten to the office when the phone rang with Browning on the line.

"Hello Chief." Jordan said.

"Yeah Jordan, what's up?"

Jordan began, "This thing went down tonight, much like the guy said it would. We have three guys in custody; they were apprehended with one of the bags in hand. They were witnessed abducting Mr. Hertwitz earlier, subsequently forcing him to reveal the location of the bags. They are to be charged with, kidnapping, resisting arrest, and terroristic theatning with the use of a fire arm. We can hold them on these charges but if you want, you can have them first."

"We definitely want them here, there are several loose ends we have to clear up." Browning assured him.

"What am I to do with Mr. Hertwitz?" Jordan Asked.

"We want him also. I don't intend to charge him with anything, but he has a lot of information which will help us tie up the loose ends," Browning said.

"He has said he will return to Marmelle voluntarily, shall I ask him to come there on his own or do you feel more comfortable sending for him?" Jordan asked.

"I'll send for him."

"Should I hold him or release him?"

"Just release him and ask him not to leave until I send for him." Browning said.

"How are we to deal with the valises?" Jordan asked Browning, "Hertzwitz doesn't have a key and they don't appear to have been opened."

"Of course, we'll want them in our possession as evidence." Browning said, "As for what's done with them after that will be up to the judge ."

"How do you want to transport them, are we to send them with your guys when they come for the prisoners?"

"No. I'll send special men in a special vehicle." Browning said.

29

After the criminals were dispensed, Cleo's attention turned to Rico.

"I should go to Rico and tell him what's happened." Cleo said to Jeb, "He has been very upset over this thing. Could you drive me by his place?"

"Certainly! Anytime you're ready." Jeb said.

"I should check with Jordan first." Cleo said.

After a brief chat with Jordan, Jeb drove to Rico's place.

"Should I wait and drive you home after you talk with Rico?" Jeb asked.

"That would be great! I might need a little help persuading Rico that it's safe at last." Cleo said.

Arriving at Rico's, Cleo knocked on the door and waited for several moments and listened for movement inside. He knocked again, still no answer. Finally, Cleo said, "Rico, it's me, your friend; please open the door." Still no sound.

"Rico, it's me, your friend from Angus, my boss is with me from the salvage yard"

Finally, Cleo heard noise from inside, "Rico scared!"

"I know you are, you'll be happy to learn the bad guys are in jail, there's no cause to be scared anymore. Please open the door and let us talk to you."

Cleo heard the sound of furniture being moved, finally Rico opened the door, an incredulous look on his face revealed the torment in his soul.

"We did it Rico!" Cleo said, "the bad guys are all in jail."

A nervous smile appeared on Rico's lips."Rico can go work now?" he asked.

"If you're ready, we'll go have to talk to Ray and see what he thinks."

"You very good friend, I ask Ray if I can work now." Rico was beginning to beam.

In an effort to add to Rico's confidence, Cleo said, "I'll go with you and explain to Ray."

"I'll drive you." Jeb said.

After explaining the situation, "He's a very good worker, I'm glad he's alright." Ray said.

30

The three men refused to answer any questions without a lawyer. They were placed in separate cells and told they would be sent back to Marmelle, none offered a comment. The police took their I.D.s: the African American had two: One showed him as an African American, D.C. 'Lucky' Wallace, the other as a Latino, Alejero Ruis. The tough looking guy was Luigi B. Gabardi,

"What does the 'B' stand for?" The officer asked.

"It stands for BEAST, and for good reason!" he said in a menacing tone.

The officer just smiled. The third guy was Harry Magness.

The van arrived to pick up the prisoners, accompanied by the driver and two armed guards. The prisoners were escorted to the van in hand cuffs and ankle bracelets. Once inside the van, their feet were also shackled to a fixed bar.

While the driver was securing the necessary paper work, a guard instructed the prisoners.

"We have about a four and half-hour ride. The van is equipped with a toilet; you may use it, one at a time, as is necessary. We'll be stopping twice, barring unforeseen problems: one for gas, the other for food. You will remain on the van while you eat. Are there any questions?" No one spoke.

The Guard continued, "You are permitted to have conversation with each other. However; for safety reasons, one of us will listen to the conversation."

Signaling the end of the rules, the guard said, "Feel free to speak to either of us if you have an emergency. Not our real names but you may call me Jim, the other guard Joe, and the driver John."

Dan Watson arrived to pick up Cleo, along with Paul Snider, as his mission was complete. Shortly thereafter the armored car, along with two armed guards, arrived to take possession of the valises. After the necessary paper work was done they were on their way to Marmelle.

Watson trailed the armored car, adding extra security. A little over 4 hours later the convoy arrived at police headquarters in Marmelle. Extra security was present as the two bags were unloaded and carried inside.

A look of anticipation was evident on Chief Browning's face as well as Cleo's. For a brief moment the two simply looked at each other.

"We meet at last!" The Chief said, " I'm Chuck Browning" offering his hand.

"It's an honor Sir." Cleo said, with just a hint of uncertainty, "I'm Cleo Hertwitz."

"We have a lot to talk about" the Chief said, "If you would rather wait until you're rested, there is no urgency."

"Well Sir, I'm alright, if you're prepared, I'll be happy to answer any question you might have, if indeed I have the answers." Cleo said.

"How did you become involved in this situation?" the chief asked.

Cleo proceeded to tell the story: how he became a homeless individual, his association with Rico, his being in the vicinity of the murders and finally what he believed was his reason for taking the bags.

"I was so scared, for several reasons: one was my fear of the policeman who had made my life so miserable." Cleo paused briefly, wondering if the Chief knew about Ruis' involvement, then continued, "next, seeing two men die before my very eyes." As Cleo talked, occasionally the Chief would nod, as though he understood and maybe agreed.

"You see, I was alone in the world at that time, no one with which to appeal for safety. As a result, maybe I felt I was not accountable."

The Chief frowned but said nothing. Cleo was a bit troubled by the Chief's reaction. After a moment of reflection, Cleo continued, "At that moment, I blamed these two men who had died in front of me for my misery. Because I had lost my wife and only son due to drug trafficking, the thought came to me, *'This will not get into the wrong hands.'*

"What were your plans for the bags?' the Chief asked.

"Benefitting from their contents was never a consideration, even right now I don't know exactly what they contain, but I'm definitely interested in knowing."

The room became very quiet, each one present engrossed in his own thoughts.

The Chief's intercom beeped, "Yes Beth?"

"I'm back—did you miss me?"

"Oh Yeah! Beth, would you step in here for a minute?"

"Yes, Sir."

As she walked into the room, Cleo almost gasped aloud. She was stunning!

"Beth, this is Cleo Hertwitz, the guy we've been chasing for a long time." Chuck said, then turned to Beth and said, "Cleo this is my right arm; we call her Beth."

Beth, in a most charming way, offered her hand and said, "Well! You certainly don't fit the description given me! It's nice to meet you Cleo Hetzwitz!"

"How do you do Beth, the pleasure is mine" Cleo said, wondering if his uneasiness was obvious.

The Chief turned and said, "Beth we are about to look inside these two valises. There's a problem--we don't have a key, you'll need to get me a locksmith down here on the double."

"Consider it done!" Beth said as she moved toward the door. As she walked past Cleo she looked at him and smiled. Cleo didn't know if he smiled back, he didn't feel comfortable trying to say anything..

After she left, Browning turned to Watson and the others and said, "I'd like for all of you to stay and witness the opening of these bags. After they're open, I'll ask each of you to sign that you were witnesses.

The smithy arrive shortly and soon had the bags open. The Chief gave off a keen whistle, "That's a lot of money!" Again the Chief called Beth, "I want you to count this money in the presence of these witnesses."

"What do I get out of this?" she asked.

"To keep your job!" Browning said jokingly.

"You're no fun." She said

Cleo could not keep his eyes off her. She picked up a bundle from the stack and counted, "Exactly one thousand dollars." She carefully took the stacks from the valise and neatly placed them on the table,

"There are one hundred and fifty stacks." Beth looked at the Chief, smiled and said, "I can get you a calculator."

"I don't think that will be necessary, Fiesty Pants!"

Everyone in the room chuckled-- everyone except Cleo that is. He was still mesmerized by the presence of Beth. All present, including Cleo, signed the form acknowledging their witness to the opening and counting of the money and seeing the drugs.

"Watson, get these bags to the evidence room, along with the witness sheet," the Chief said, "And Beth, get Mr. Hertzwitz a voucher for his stay with us: his meals, and his return trip to St Ann."

The chief turned to Cleo, "Do you mind traveling by bus?"

"No, of course not." Cleo quickly responded.

"You are permitted to return to your job, but it's mandatory that you report to us once a week. You can do that by phone," the Chief said."you're not being charged at this time and we don't anticipate forth coming charges, but our investigation is not complete."

Still a little nervous from it all, Cleo said, "Thank you sir, I understand and I'll gladly comply."

Cleo looked at Beth in spite of himself, only to discover she had been listening intently to it all. She smiled and said, "Mister Cleo Hertzwitz, looks like you and I have a standing date." Cleo responded in some way but wasn't sure what he said.

31

Cleo decided to wait 'til the next day to return to St Ann. He called Jeb and told him.

"Sure," Jeb said, "take as much time as you need"

Ironically, Cleo decided to go to the Black Angus Steakhouse for dinner.

He ordered a t-bone steak with baked potato, peach cobbler and coffee.

As he ate his dinner and pondered the recent events of his life, disbelief filled his thoughts. The transition from tramp to witness was almost as incredible as the event which made him a tramp in the first place. Ah, the irony of it all!

He couldn't keep from thinking of Beth. Everything about her was most charming: the way she put everyone around her at ease, the re-assuring smile, her wittiness.

After all that had happened to him, Maggie seemed like such a long time ago.

His thoughts brought him back to reality: *What have I to offer a woman? Mostly penniless-- a junkyard jocky? A recent tramp, wanted by the authorities?*

Still, his need for female companionship was abruptly aroused.

"Would you like more coffee, sir?" the waitress asked.

Cleo was startled by the question. It was then he realized he had eaten very little of his dinner.

"Yes, please," feeling sheepish, he began to finish his steak.

After an uneventful return trip to St. Ann, Cleo was surprised to find Jeb and Patty waiting at the terminal for his arrival.

"How would you like to go to Ricky's and have dinner? My treat? You can bring us up to date," Jeb asked.

"I'd like that very much." Cleo replied.

It was obvious they were anxious to learn of what had taken place.

"How'd it go?" Jeb asked, as they were being seated.

"Everything went very well," Cleo said, then proceeded to relate the course of events: getting a locksmith to open the valises, the counting of the money, the security surrounding the area. Finally, realizing they wanted to know what was in the bags, he told of the lady who is the Chief's secretary, methodically counting and sorting several stacks.

"One hundred and fifty thousand dollars. Wow! That's a lot of dough! It's no wonder these thugs wanted to get their hands on it." Jeb said, tilting his head back and raising his eyebrows, smiling, "We could've bought a lot of junk with that!"

"The other bag contained what looked like powdered sugar," Cleo Continued, "but I suspect it was something very different from powdered sugar."

"How were you received?" Patty asked.

"Very well indeed! There were no congratulations of course, and I have to report once a week, but I can do that by phone and the Chief said he didn't expect there would be any charges coming to me," Cleo said with a very obvious feeling of relief.

"How about Tony?" Cleo asked.

"We haven't seen him!" Patty said, "Do you think he had something to do with what went down?"

"OH yes!" Cleo said emphatically, "He ran like a rat when the thugs grabbed me. Besides, he has never been the slightest bit friendly toward me, and the fact that he offered to buy my supper that night convinced me he was leading me to the gallows and that put me on guard."

Cleo couldn't get Beth off his mind. Monday he call, "Good morning Beth, this is Cleo Hertwitz calling in."

"Well! Good morning Cleo Hertwitz, how are you today?"

"I'm fine, thank you, but I'm not sure what I'm supposed to say? Maybe-- I'm here but my heart is in Marmelle?" Cleo said, audibly chuckling.

"It's a good place to leave your heart," She said.

After a brief pause, she continued, "The boss told me your story, may I say, I'm sorry."

"Thank you, what about yourself? Are there good things in your life"?

"Oh, you wouldn't want to know about me," she said.

"I think I would. Maybe before this thing is over we'll have an opportunity to tell each other our stories," Cleo said .

After what seemed like 10 minutes, Beth finally said, "I'd like that."

"Well, I'll call you again next week."

Again there was a short lull, "I look forward to it-- goodbye."

The call left him bewildered, *Did something I said disturb her? Was she re-living some event in her life? Was that her way of saying 'Lay off Buddy?*

Maybe I should let her make the next move.

✳

The next day as Jeb and Cleo were finishing their lunch, Cleo decided to approach Jeb with an idea.

"Jeb, I'd like to talk to someone in Marmelle concerning a recovery center for drug addicted individuals, the homeless, and individuals who are temporarily disturbed mentally. What do you think our chances are of creating such an interest?"

"Probably little and likely none."

"The money recovered from the druggies could be used toward such a project. Of course, that amount of money would be insignificant considering the cost of securing the facility and future maintenance. It would require many volunteers. However; I believe with individual, city, county, and state contributions it could be done." Cleo reasoned.

"That's a noble idea, one that's badly needed. But—I have to warn you, even if you got some interest going, the odds are against it ever coming to fruition. I'm sorry if I've dampened you ambition. If this is your passion—Go for it! Since I've come to know you, I think you can do anything."

"Later on, I'd like to talk to the chief there to see if he would consider it."

Rico came to bus the table, "How do you like working for Ray?" Cleo asked,

"Ray say Rico do good work, he like very much. Maybe give me more money soon."

"I don't think I've told you how much I appreciate your help in catching the crooks," Cleo said as he extended his hand and took Rico's.

With a big smile, "Cleo very good friend." With that Rico disappeared into the kitchen.

32

Each Monday Cleo called in to report. For the last several weeks, Beth had not been the jolly, fun-filled person. Cleo was bewildered by the change and decided her interest in him was probably all his imagination.

"Hi Beth, this is Cleo Hertzwitz. Is there anything going on concerning the jailbirds?"

"They have several charges against them: possession of drugs with fire arms involved, threatening police officers and kidnapping of the restaurant worker. There are others but these guys are going down for a long time." Beth still seemed distant.

Cleo's curiosity overcame him, "Beth you seem different when we talk now."

"What do you mean?"

"I don't know, you seemed so jolly and carefree when I met you."

"Well, I have my days."

"I'm sorry, I shouldn't have asked." Cleo stammered.

"It's alright, I'm happy you asked. Don't forget, we have a date to talk about our past."

"I haven't forgotten and I look forward with great anticipation to that date." Cleo said, feeling somewhat relieved.

As Cleo and Jeb were finishing lunch, Cleo decided to approach Jeb with the idea of his buying himself a car. It had been so long since he had his driver's license renewed, he wasn't sure what that would entail. Uneasily he turned to Jeb and said, "Jeb, it's time I got me some wheels. What do I need to do to get my license, and how do I go about getting a car? I have a little money but not enough to buy a very good one."

"Well first, let's see about the car; if you fail at that you won't need a license."

"What do you suggest" Cleo asked.

"I'll co-sign with you, but you're going to be asked for previous credit." Jeb said.

"Well you know I have no recent credit history. I had very good credit before everything collapsed."

"Do you think they would give you a favorable recommendation at your bank where you lived before all this happened?"

"Well, I feel sure they would. One day soon I'll give the bank president a call and see what he suggests," Cleo said.

"There's never a better time than right now," Jeb suggested

Cleo picked up the phone and called the bank. "Hello, this is Cleo Hertzwitz, I'd like to speak with your president Jeff Hubbard please."

"Just a moment please."

Jeff picked up the receiver. "Hello, this is Jeff Hubbard, how may I help you."

"Mr. Hubbard, this is Cleo Hertswitz, I-----

Jeff interrupted, "Cleo? Cleo Herzwitz? I thought you had surely died. We've been trying to find you since the tragedy; there are some funds on record here in Maggie's name. It seems she was making regular deposits for Chad's college. Also, she had a life insurance policy on him. We'd like to get with you and clear up this matter

Cleo was unable to say a word.

"Are you still there?" Jeff asked.

"Yes-----Yes sure----I'm still here. I'm so shocked by what you've just told me. How much money are you talking about?" Cleo stammered.

"Just a moment," Jeff paged the secretary, "Susan, bring me the files on Cleo Hertzwitz. You'll find them in the 'pending files'."

After a momentary pause, Jeff said, "I'm sorry for the wait. Let's see--- the college fund, including accrued interest to date comes to $13,732.15—the life policy is for $50,000.00. Since the policy was purchased through the bank, we'll be able to handle the entire matter here."

"Is it necessary for me to make an appointment?" Cleo asked.

"Not at all. Our hours are 9 to 5 Monday through Friday, we'll be happy to accommodate you at your convenience."

"Since I'm several miles away, I'll call before I come. For now I have to put myself back together after learning of what you've just told me."

"Very well. You've not told me why you called." Jeff said.

"It's nothing that won't wait. Thank you so much, I'll be in touch."

Cleo turned to Jeb and sat speechless.

Finally Jeb, thinking he had received more bad news said, "What on earth is it Cleo?!"

"I'm going to tell you, but again you're not going to believe it. The banker I was about to ask for a loan just told me I have several thousand dollars waiting for me there. It seems Maggie had been putting away money for Chad's college, of which I had no knowledge. I suppose she intended for it to be a surprise to me when the time came. Also, along with the account, she had purchased a sizeable life insurance policy."

"Well, this changes things considerably," Jeb sighed.

"Yes it does," Cleo quickly responded, "But nothing in this world will ever change between you and me."

The two sat for a few minutes mulling over the situation.

Finally, Cleo broke the silence, "Jeb I have no idea how things will turn out for me during and after the trial. I'll have to be gone for a few weeks while the trial is going on. Lawyers have a way of making the truth sound like a lie.

Jeb, placing his hand on Cleo's shoulder, said, "Cleo, Patty and I have known for a long time something of your potential and certainly you belong somewhere besides a salvage yard handy man. I am so glad to have had a part in your recovery. I hope you find your place, but if something doesn't go just right, you'll always have someone to turn to."

"I keep remembering those cold, lonely nights in that hole in the ground in Marmelle and the nightmares that came much too often;" Cleo said, "I keep thinking I'll wake up and all this will have been just another dream."

Cleo paused a moment, considering how to proceed, "I plan to go to Paramore as soon as possible and see to the business there. I'm sure there will be some gathering of information, such as death certificates, for both Maggie and Chad, that may take a few days."

"Take as much time as you need, we'll be fine at the yard," Jeb said.

The next day Cleo called the Chief's office in Marmelle. Beth answered. "How are things going ?" he asked.

"The Sun Also Rises in Marmelle, how's it with you?" she said.

"I have just been informed I have to go back to my old home town to take care of some business there. I expect to be gone a few days. I'd like to get permission to wait until I return to report in, as I won't have access to a private phone. Will there be a problem with that?"

"I don't think so, I'll get with the Chief and let you know," Beth said. "Let me have your number and I'll get back to you."

True to her word, Beth called shortly, "The Chief said there would be no problem. Call me when you get back."

"That I will do. Thanks Beth."

Then Cleo called the bank in Paramore notifying them he was on his way, to settle his business there. He boarded the bus at 9 a.m. The ride to Paramore took five hours, arriving at 2 p.m. The first order of business was getting something to eat, after which he went to the bank.

"May I help you?" the young teller asked.

I'm Cleo Hertzwitz. I'd like to speak with Jeff Hubbard please. I believe he is expecting me.

"One moment please," pushing Jeff's number,

"Yes?"

"A Mister Cleo Hertzwitz to see you sir."

"Please ask him to come in."

"Come with me please," the teller said as she went into the lobby, leading the way to Jeff's office.

"Cleo! It's good to see you again. We were fearful something dreadful had happened to you." Jeff said as he grabbed Cleo's hand.

The thought came to Cleo, *if he only knew,*

"Well, it's good to see you sir."

"Would you like a cup of coffee?" Jeff asked.

"No thank you, I'll not take a lot of your time if you would like to get started."

Leaning back, Jeff added, "I don't have a busy schedule this afternoon, why not relax and tell me what you've been doing."

"I'm not really sure you want to know, it's a very long story."

Cleo told of the events of his life since the death of his wife and son.

Jeff sat, listening intently as Cleo spoke. Finally Cleo got to his recent call to the bank.

"I needed to buy a car and of course I had no recent credit. Jeb, my boss, offered to co-sign with me but felt the bank there would want to know something about me. I called to ask if you would give me a favorable recommendation. Truthfully, I wasn't sure what to expect. You can only imagine my surprise to learn of what you've told me."

Jeff smiled, "I imagine you'll want the balance of the savings account in cash. However, there is a process which we must follow to actually get the funds from the insurance company. That won't be a problem, it's just that procedure must be followed. The $13,000.00 should be enough to buy a pretty nice used car and when all is cleared, I'll forward the insurance money to wherever you say."

Cleo paused, "For safety reasons, I'd like for you to advance me $1000.00 cash from the savings account now, when I get back to St. Ann I'll call you and give the necessary account information."

"That's a good idea, why not get that done right away?" Jeff said.

Cleo nodded "I'd like that. As far as my buying a car, I'll have to wait until I have obtained my license to do that."

Jeff buzzed someone, "Bring a withdrawal slip and an authorization form to my office please."

Shortly a young lady arrived with the form. "Sign right here, Cleo, and she'll bring you your money. Sign this authorization form , which will give us power of attorney to dispense these funds."

"Would you like all big bills?" the young lady asked.

"If you don't mind, give me $100.00 in smaller bills."

"Yes sir." She said and left the office, returning momentarily with nine $100.00 bills and five $20's.

"Let me hear from you from time to time, Cleo, I'm more than a little interested in your recovery, it's an incredible story."

"Thank you Jeff, I'll do just that," Cleo said. He shook hands with Jeff and left the bank for the bus station.

There wasn't another bus for St. Ann for 2 ½ hours. Cleo decided to get a cab and cruise the old neighborhood.

"Stop here," Cleo said.

Everything looked much like it did when he left, except the rubbish of Chad's house and the neighbor's .That had been cleared away. The place looked bare with the buildings gone. Memories began flooding his mind. Remembering Chad as a young boy romping in the back yard, Maggie yelling, 'Watch where you're going.' The private times he and Maggie had together. Life was so good then. Still it seemed so long ago and far away. In spite of the memories, he didn't feel the attachment as much as he thought he would.

He didn't feel comfortable leaving the cab and walking around, thinking it would be awkward if he should happen to meet some of the former neighbors.

"Sir, the meter is running," the cabbie said, jolting Cleo back to the present.

"Thank you, I'm ready to return to the bus station."

Back at the station, he bought a local paper and settled in for the 2 hour wait for the bus.

Arriving at St Ann at 10:15, Cleo decided to walk to the boarding house, not only to stretch his legs but time enough to consider what lay ahead.

He arose early the next morning, Cleo decided to pass up breakfast at the boarding house. He walked to the salvage yard, stopping on the way at the fast food restaurant for a breakfast sandwich and a cup of coffee. Arriving at work early, he let himself in and opened the office.

Arriving shortly thereafter, Jeb said, "Well! This is a surprise, we didn't expect you back for a couple of days,"

"With power of attorney, the bank agreed to take care of most of the details, without my being present. Eventually they will forward the funds," Cleo said. "I didn't feel comfortable riding a bus with a lot of cash, so I only took $1000.00 of the savings in order to establish an account here, to which the remainder of the funds may be deposited."

"Well, we still haven't resolved the problem of obtaining your driver's license and buying a car."

"First things first," Cleo said, "Tomorrow I'll go to the revenue office and get the process started."

The next day Cleo began the process at the bank.

"Good morning, I'm Cleo Hertzwitz; who do I see about opening an account?" Cleo asked the teller.

"I'll take you to Ms. Simmons' office-- follow me please."

"Ms. Simmons, this is Cleo Hertzwitz, he's interested in opening an account with us."

"Good morning Mr. Hertzwitz, I'm Claire Simmons, please have a seat.

Now how can I help you?"

"Ms. Simmons, I've been out of circulation for quite a long time, matter of fact I've been homeless during this time. I can give you the boring details if you think it's necessary."

"Have you been in trouble with the law?" Ms. Simmons asked.

"No, it's nothing like that; it's just that I don't have an immediate background that can be researched. I have been working for Jeb Clancy at his salvage yard for a few weeks now, he knows of my immediate past and will vouch for my integrity."

"I don't think that will be necessary. Are you looking to open a checking or savings account?" Simmons asked.

"Checking, for now." He said.

"For now? What do you mean?"

"I only have a small amount today, but in a few days there will be more arriving to be deposited to this account. Soon there will be a much larger sum forthcoming, the proceeds of a life insurance policy. I will want to open a savings account for that." Cleo explained.

"We can open the checking today and when the remainder of your money comes here, we can deposit it to this account, later you can open the savings account and transfer as much as you want. How does that sound?"

"That'll be fine," He said. "I need to buy a car; how long must I wait to actually write a check?" He asked.

"Are you depositing cash or other---"

"It's cash," Cleo interrupted.

"Then you may write checks tomorrow," She said.

After obtaining the pertinent information, Ms. Simmos asked, "How much do you want to deposit today?"

" $900.00."

Simmons made and gave Cleo a deposit slip along with a few computer-created checks. "Thank you, Mr. Hertzwitz, we appreciate your banking with us."

"Thank you, it's been a pleasure." Cleo said. He shook hands with Simmons and left the bank.

The process for obtaining a driver's license took much longer. Because his license had been expired for so long, he was required to take a driver's test which was only given one day each week. Eventually he succeeded and became a legitimate driver.

That business complete, he called the bank in Paramore and gave them the account number to which the remainder of the account there was to be transferred.

A few days later Cleo received a deposit slip for $12,780.38

The following Saturday Jeb and Cleo went car shopping. After considerable haggling and $6,595.00 later, Cleo had his wheels. The following Monday he obtained insurance.

Back at the yard, Cleo, nervously approached Jeb. "Jeb, if I take a few days off, will it put you in a bind?"

"Oh, I can manage very well—what do you have on your mind?"

"I want to go to Marmelle and talk to the chief about some things. I want to feel him out concerning the project we talked about. I need to know how the trial of the three men is coming along and find out what role I'm likely to have in it." Cleo was careful not to mention the real reason he was going to Marmelle.

"Cleo, you have a job here as long as you want it. You've been as much help to me as I have for you. I've learned many things since you've been here---something of the human spirit. I have witnessed a transition few men will ever see, I'm glad to have had a part in it. But, recognizing your potential, I urge you to continue your recovery by finding a more productive occupation back into the everyday walks of life," Chuckling, "maybe even find a new Ms. Hertzwitz."

Cleo wondered if his expression revealed something that caused Jeb to make that remark.

Cleo called in to report and as usual Beth was her enthusiastic self, "Good morning, or is it afternoon?"

"Well, it's afternoon but who's watching the clock?" Cleo said, "I have purchased some wheels for myself. I intend to be in Marmelle

Wednesday, I'd like to talk to the Chief about something. I wonder if you could secure me an appointment with him, say around 2-3 o'clock?"

"Oh, he's seldom busy, but I'll get you confirmed. Is your business something you'd like to share with me, or shall I keep him in the dark?"

"I don't mind sharing, it concerns an idea. I want to ask him if he would entertain an idea of a recovery center for druggies, alcoholics, in some cases, homeless folks and if the money confiscated from the jail birds could be used."

"Sounds like a great idea!" Beth said.

Feeling somewhat like going for broke, afraid of losing everything, Cleo asked, "Would you like to have dinner with me Wednesday evening?"

There was a lull, and Cleo's throat became very dry. "If you'd rather not, I'll understand, perhaps I shouldn't have asked." Still the lull continued. Cleo was about to abandon the idea altogether,

Then Beth said, "Cleo, I'd be honored to have dinner with you Wednesday. 7 o'clock be alright?"

"Give me your home address and I'll pick you up at 7" Cleo said, a very warm glow came over him.

Cleo stopped off at the phone company and purchased his cell phone and left for Marmelle.

What will I talk about? Certainly not my recent history; there's nothing interesting about the junk business. I have no family, no pictures of grandkids.

The closer he came to Marmelle, the sweatier his hands became. He arrived shortly after lunch and gave Beth a call.

"Good afternnon Beth, this is Cleo."

"Well, and good afternoon to you Mr. Cleo!" Her cheery voice made him even more nervous.

"Do I have an appointment?" Cleo asked, wondering if his anxiety was being transmitted in his voice.

"I spoke to the Chief and he said you could meet with him at your convenience."

"I'm in town now; I'll eat lunch, and then I'll be in to see him," Cleo said. "Will two 0'clock be alright.?

"Certainly, enjoy your lunch," said Beth.

Beth rang the Chief's office, "Cleo Hertzwitz is here. Shall I send him in?"

"By all means." the Chief said. Extending his hand Cleo said, "Good afternoon sir, it's good to see you

again."

"Come in Cleo, have a seat."

"Thank you, sir.

"What is it you want to see me about?" the Chief asked.

"You are aware of my immediate past and as you might expect, I know something of the misery and agony displaced people endure. I'd like to ask your opinion on establishing a center for such people here in Marmelle. Of course, I don't know who has the authority to dispense confiscated funds such as those acquired from what has just taken place here but if enough interest could be raised, maybe part of it could be used for that."

"Cleo, I've talked at length with the chief in St. Ann. I must say, what you did there is certainly to be commended. You amaze me in so many ways."

The chief paused, Cleo thought *"He's about to tell me to mind my own business and be thankful I'm not in jail with the others."*

The Chief continued, "I don't know who has the authority to

dispense these funds. It's my understanding after the judge awards the money, it becomes city property. If that's the case, I suppose it would become the city council's responsibility. I'll say this, you have a commendable idea and I, for one, would be for looking into it further." Cleo was encouraged by the Chief's support.

He then asked, "What is the status of the three men that were arrested?"

"They have been arraigned, pled not guilty and a trial date has been set," The Chief said, "A bond has been set, but none have been able to make it. Due to the nature of the crimes, the judge set their bond at $1,000,000.00 each. They will be tried separately, we hope one of them will give us some information concerning the source of the drugs being brought to Marmelle in exchange for a lighter sentence."

Reluctantly Cleo said, "Chief, when this thing is over, I'm going to have to find a job. Do you have any suggestions?

"Are you planning to move to Marmelle? The Chief asked.

"Yes Sir." Cleo said.

"What kind of job are you looking for?" the Chief asked. "what kind of work were you engaged in before all this happened?"

"I was the personnel manager for a manufacturing company. I worked there for 12 years, 8 of which I held that position."

"Well, I don't know of a manufacturer that's looking for a personnel manager, but there are some places I can ask around, maybe find something to your liking," the Chief said, smiling.

"Thank you Chief, I'm in no position to be too choosy, I appreciate your help. With regards to the center I mentioned, if we can create enough interest, I'm willing to donate all the time I can spare to its creation and maintenance."

Cleo took a note pad and wrote his cell number, stood and handed it to the Chief and said, "If something arises concerning the three, I'll be nearby. Thank you for seeing me," and he offered his hand.

Taking Cleo's hand the Chief said, "There is no longer a need for you to report. I wish you luck Cleo. Good afternoon."

After leaving the Chief, he stopped at Beth's desk, "Are we still on for tonight?" he asked.

"Unless you've changed *your* mind, we are still on," she said.

"I'm new in town---well, I'm new in the social world of Marmelle, where shall we go for dinner?" Cleo asked.

"How about the Angus?" she asked.

"Very appropriate! Seven then?"

Cleo arrived promptly at 7 and rang the bell. Beth answered the door and asked if he would like to come in.

"Well, maybe we should go. I have asked for a table that affords the greater privacy," Cleo said.

"Good!" she said as they walked to his car. "Those are nice wheels—did you have a bag you didn't tell us about?"

"Not exactly, but I have something to tell you."

After being seated and placing their order, Cleo said, "I have to confess, it's been a long time since I've entertained a lady friend, so if my etiquette is out of sync with today's world, maybe you could either overlook my stumbling or give me some tips."

"I promise not to hold you to any standards—I may be as out of touch as you claim to be." Beth assured him.

During the meal Cleo told of receiving his unexpected wealth, buying the car and Jeb encouraging him to look for better employment.

"So, are you planning to move here?" she asked.

"I spoke to the chief about that possibility. He said that he might be of assistance in helping me find a suitable job. I was personnel manager for a manufacturing firm in Paramore for several years. I don't expect to be interviewed for such a job, but there are several other positions for which I might qualify."

After completeing the meal the waiter brought the wine and asked if they cared for some.

Cleo looked at Beth and said, "Let's"

"Why not?"she asked. The waiter poured and left.

As they sipped the wine, silence set in, both realizing what was surely to be coming; neither wanted to be first.

Finally Beth broke the silence, "It's hard for me to realize I'm having dinner with a man who doesn't even know my last name."

"That's no problem —Beth is just fine." Cleo said.

"No, it's not O.K. My name is Beth Janson. There was a Mr. Janson, his name was Johnny. He and I grew up together and were class mates. I'm not sure exactly when we began to be interested in each other in a special way. Eventually we realized we were in love and wanted to be together. The day we graduated from high school we got married. For four years we were the happiest couple in all the world."

Suddenly she got very quiet, Cleo wondered what to expect next.

Finally, she continued, "One night three thugs broke into our house with guns drawn, demanding money. We gave them what we had, hoping they would leave. Instead, one of them grabbed me and began to tear my clothes. When Johnny assaulted the man, one of the others shot him. The picture of Johnny falling back, grasping his chest, lying in such a way as to be looking directly at me--- I'll never, ever forget the look in Johnny's eyes as they were gently closing forever. His eyes seemed to be screaming, HELP ME!, HELP ME! Finally I realized it was me who was doing the screaming."

Beth reached for a tissue as tears welled up. She wasn't able to continue right away.

Cleo reached and took her hand, at which Beth quickly and instinctively withdrew. Then, as though she realized what she had done, quickly took Cleo's hand and gave a light squeeze. Again she wiped away the persistent tears.

Again Cleo reached for her hand, "Beth, if you rather not......."

"Please let me finish. After they shot Johnny, they took turns raping and hitting me. They didn't just rape my body, they raped me of my dreams of a future life, of having children and grandchildren: they raped me of my confidence and security. They raped me of the husband whom I adored and all the prospects which that relationship promised."

Beth paused for several moments. Cleo became uncomfortable but not knowing what to say, remained silent. Beth's agony was apparent.

Finally she continued, "At some point I lost consciousness and woke up in a psychiatric ward and was told I had been unresponsive for four days. I was confined to that hospital for two weeks during which time I saw a psychiatrist twice a day. Following my dismissal from the hospital, I continued to see the doctor once a week for two years. He finally told me he had done all he could for me."Again she grew silent. Finally,"Men became the epitome of evil. When I saw a man-- any man, I'd just freak out. You once expressed concern about my attitude, and I promised to explain. Well, now you know. My jolly presence is my way of dealing with those dreadful memories. I reckon I can't explain my attraction to you. For the first time in many years I feel a little like shedding my guard."

Cleo sat, absolutely absorbed in what Beth was saying. Several moments passed before either spoke. Finally, Beth took her glass and put it to her lips. Her hands were shaking so, it was difficult not to spill its contents.

Cleo finally spoke,"Beth, I'm so sorry. There is a line in a song which I think speaks to the both of us; it says, *"The truth is the hardest thing in the world to face, 'cause you can't change the truth in the slightest way."*

He paused to see how she re-acted. "Friends say such things as, *This too will pass* or *Life goes on,* or *You just have to pick up the pieces and go on* or *Time heals all wounds.* Believe me, I've heard them all. I believe people mean to be helpful, but there is no help. Each personal tragedy belongs to that person alone, and it is he/she that must ultimately deal with it."

To that Beth replied, "I know that, however; I find it very difficult to put confidence in anything. I feel so deprived because of that feeling. To know something and to realize something are two different things altogether. You know I'm hurting; I know you're hurting, but because I'm not you, I can't realize your pain; the same is with me."

Again Beth picked up her wine glass, this time her hands were much calmer.

Cleo smiled and said, "I'm more than a little honored by your taking me into your confidence and sharing these things with me, it must have been difficult. I hope by venting, as you have, some inner peace will come."

This time, Beth took Cleo's hand, "Johnny has been gone 8 years and I have not spoken this way since. I really can't explain it. I thank you for listening."

"Would you care for more wine?" Cleo asked.

"No, I'm fine. We still have some daylight, how'd you like to drive to the park and take a walk?" Beth asked.

Somewhat surprised, Cleo said, "A wonderful idea!"

At the park they walked side by side, neither spoke. Cleo, supposing Beth needed quiet time after re-living the events in her life, was happy to remain silent.

As they continued their walk, Beth took Cleo's hand but said nothing.

At last they were at Beth's steps.

"Cleo, thank you for a wonderful evening; this has meant so much to me."

Slightly stammering, Cleo said, "Well, I don't know quite what to say. I feel like I've known you my whole life, and I too have had a most enjoyable evening. I'd like to do it again soon."

"It's unavoidable. " Beth said in her witty way.

33

The return trip to St Ann seemed so short this time. The thoughts of Beth were like gentle breezes propelling his cloud.

Arriving at the salvage yard, he greeted the Clancys. "Let's have dinner at Ricky's, it's my treat this time."

"We can be ready in twenty minutes, does that sound O.K.?" Jeb asked.

"Absolutely!"

After being seated, Jeb said, "How'd your new car perform?"

"It did very well indeed, even my date liked it." Cleo said as a way of introducing the fact he'd had a lady friend for dinner.

"OH! We had a date with a lady friend," Patty said mockingly.

"Her name is Beth Jansen," Cleo said, "she works for the police chief in Marmelle. It was a most interesting evening."

"How was the idea of the center received," Jeb asked.

"The chief is the only person I was able to speak with concerning the project, but he was very much interested and promised to look into it more fully."

Cleo drew quiet, reluctant to introduce the next subject, "I spoke to the chief concerning a job there in Marmelle, he has promised to ask around." No one spoke right away.

"We're happy for you and hope things work out on all fronts, especially with the lady friend," Jeb said.

"She's a delightful person. She has had a very traumatic event occur in her life and has some real emotional scars as a result," Cleo said. Leaning across the table he continued, "Jeb and Patty! I can't adequately express my feeling for the two of you. I can't imagine what would have become of me if I hadn't met you. I can only hope that I may be able to help someone else sometime as you have helped me."

Feeling a little more comfortable now that the subject was opened, Cleo said, "I will stay and help you until you are completely satisfied with whoever takes my place."

"Cleo, you stay as long as you want or leave when you're ready, we'll be fine. You have been an inspiration to us as well. I can only say that I'm glad I didn't go with my instincts when I first saw you." Jeb said, smiling

Patty chimed in, "I too, have had a major change of impression, I couldn't believe Jeb had taken you on--------but I'm very glad he did."

She opened her purse, pulled out an envelope and said,

"This came for you today."

Cleo laid it beside him as if to continue the conversation,

"Go on, open it, we're curious. " Beth urged.

A deposit slip for $50,000.00, the proceeds from the life insurance policy.

Cleo sit staring at the paper,

"How can I explain this?! I thought 'From Rags to Riches' was a cliché, or maybe a line of a song. I never dreamed it could actually happen to regular people." Cleo looked up from the paper, "I owe this good fortune to you two as well. As you have said, your first thought was to tell me to get lost, the fact that you didn't has given me a second chance at life."

"Cleo, when a person has a part in making good things happen, it creates a feeling that can't be compared to money," Jeb said. "Your good fortune has created just such a feeling for Patty and me."

Rico came to their table to say hello. "Ray give Rico much more money. Ray is good man."

"Rico, I'll soon be leaving St. Ann and moving back to Marmelle. I'm very happy for you and I'll keep in touch. I'll always remember the delicious meals you brought me from the Angus."

"You good friend!" Rico said and began cleaning away the table.

34

Cleo was up early next morning. He left the boarding house for the cafeteria, had breakfast and then went on the salvage yard. Due to the recent events, Patty had been helping out in the office. Cleo chatted with her for a few minutes as he waited for the bank to open. He sat there for awhile with a sad feeling welling up inside him, he couldn't conceal how he felt. After a firm handshake from Jeb and a big hug from Patty, he turned away quickly before his teary eyes became apparent. It was so difficult to say goodbye to Jeb and Patty. They had been such a part of his salvation. He gave them one last hug and left the office, drove to the boarding house, loaded his pitifully few belongings into his car, settled his rent bill, and went on to the bank. Cleo asked for a cashier's check for the balance of the account, expressed his gratitude, and with that, Cleo Hertzwitz left St. Ann.

Even though it was difficult saying goodbye to Jeb and Patty, Cleo felt it was the right thing to do, since all the events of his recent past had their origin in Marmelle. His opportunities for better employment seemed to be in Marmelle. There was a chance he'd be involved in the trial should it come to that. Everything considered, Marmelle was the most practical place to be. He couldn't lie to himself concerning the real reason he wanted to be in Marmelle.

As he headed toward Marmelle, he picked up the phone and made the call,"This is Cleo Hertzwitz calling to see how the city is fairing without me."

"This is a police department—are you in some kind of trouble?" Beth asked in her jolly manner.

"I haven't been out of trouble in a long time."

"How are you today Cleo Hertzwitz?"

"I'm in my car enroute to Marmelle with everything I own. The last time I was moving with all my earthly possessions, I wasn't quite as optimistic as I am today, thanks to the likes of you," Cleo said, as his mind drifted back.

"Do you intend to live here?" She asked.

"Yes I do and I will need to find an apartment today; do you know of something that's available?" He asked.

"Call me when you get into town, meanwhile I'll check around." Beth suggested.

"I'm still a couple of hours away--I'll call you." Cleo said and hung up.

Cleo gave Beth another call as he came into town.

"Meet me at the office, I'm about finished for the day," She said.

"There some nice apartments on Berkley, we can look there first if you'd like."

After checking several apartment complexes, Cleo decided on one, "I'll have to wait until tomorrow to actually rent. Most of my funds are in the form of a cashier's check; I'll have to establish an account. Still apprehensive, "Would you like to have dinner?" He asked cheerfully.

"I should go tidy up a bit first." Beth said smiling.

"Fine, I'll get registered at the motel. Give me a call when you're ready and I'll pick you up."

The conversation was casual while they ate. After the table was cleared, with his hands on the table, heart in his throat, Cleo began, "Beth I want to tell you what's on my mind; I ask you to let me finish before you respond. Let me begin by saying I want to spend the rest of my life with you! However; there is a possible obstacle. After my wife and son died and the ordeal with the courts, I sorta died as well. It was like being in a brilliantly lighted room, then having all the light suddenly taken away. For many months I had no communication with the real world. I had no one I cared for; no one with whom to visit or discuss anything. I had no female companionship, neither wanting it. It wasn't until I met Jeb and Patty Clancy that I began to return to life. The day I saw you for the first time, a yearning returned that actually took me by surprise."

As he continued, he noticed tears welling up in Beth's eyes, his heart nearly failed him, thinking she was about decline his approach. Realizing he was too far into this discussion to quit now, he continued, "The obstacle to which I refer is a question, *'Is the way I feel geniune or opportunistic?'* The last thing in the world I want to do is trifle with your emotions or take advantage of your emotional state. If for any reason you feel this is not right, let's not do it."

Beth gently placed her hand in his, "Cleo, we aren't teenagers. The feeling you've expressed is not 'puppy love', we both have experienced loneliness, not only loneliness, but being alone. As we both know, that's a terrible state of mind.

I think the thing that concerns you is the short time we've known each other.

The fact that you're concerned is evidence of sincerity. Much of what you've expressed is much like what I would say about my past and my loneliness and my inability to trust.

For the longest time, Beth simply looked into his eyes. Realizing this was making him uncomfortable, she continued, " Cleo Hertzwitz---if what you' ve just said is something of a marriage proposal" ---- she paused, for what seemed to Cleo to be about a week----- "then I accept."

"Beth Janson, you've made me a very happy man." He said.

"Beth Janson??? I like Beth Hertzwitz much better."

One year later, as Beth and Cleo stood gazing through the glass at the new-borns, (Johnny Chad Hertzwitz being among them) Cleo took Beth's hand and said, "It was a long way down and even further back . Having you with me, whatever is left will be smooth sailing. I love you Beth Hertzwitz.